SKELETONS!

Suddenly, Brian froze. He stopped stark-still, trembling so hard he almost fell. Along the side of the cave, he saw what had caught his eye.

Bones!

Skeletons!

Brian couldn't count them, there were so many. He forced himself to be brave. Tried to ignore the skeletons—but he couldn't.

He hadn't looked far when his flashlight flickered. He slapped it against his hand, but it didn't come back on. It was no use. The batteries were dead. His light was gone!

He was alone in the dark. Alone with the skeletons of the dead. Trapped in the dark, silent tomb of Death Cave!

Books by Bill Wallace

A DOG CALLED KITTY
TRAPPED IN DEATH CAVE

Available from ARCHWAY paperbacks

TRAPPED IN DEATH CAVE

Bill Wallace

AN ARCHWAY PAPERBACK
Published by POCKET BOOKS • NEW YORK

An Archway Paperback published by
POCKET BOOKS, a division of Simon & Schuster, Inc.
1230 Avenue of the Americas, New York, N.Y. 10020

Published by arrangement with Holiday House, Inc.
Library of Congress Catalog Card Number: 83-48962

ISBN: 0-671-62851-8

First Archway Paperback printing June, 1985

10 9 8 7 6 5

AN ARCHWAY PAPERBACK and colophon are
registered trademarks of Simon & Schuster, Inc.

Printed in the U.S.A.

IL 4+

To
WILLIAM FOSTER-HARRIS
BEE NASH
E. B. TURLEY
My teachers—my friends

TRAPPED IN DEATH CAVE

CHAPTER 1

Brian stuck his little fingers against the corners of his mouth and whistled as loud as he could. He listened. There was no answer but the rustling of the Oklahoma wind through the pear tree by the cabin. So he tried it again. This time, his whistle was so loud and piercing, it made his eyes scrunch up.

Still nothing. No one appeared at the door of the big house across from his cabin. No whistle came back to his ears from the rough, rocky slopes of the hills. Finally, he shrugged and walked back down the steps.

Mama met him right near the bottom. "Must be out playing football," she said, peeking over the big box of bed sheets in her arms.

"Must be," Brian agreed.

Dad was digging stuff out of the car trunk. For a second, it reminded Brian of somebody getting eaten by a shark. The way the trunk lid gaped open like a big jaw, and the way Dad was stuck inside, with only his bottom sticking up and his legs dangling out.

Dad finally got the ice chest he was fighting with. He made kind of a grunting sound as he wrestled it out of the trunk and got his feet on the ground again.

"Gary coming?"

Brian shrugged. "Must be off playing football or something. I whistled, but . . ."

Dad made another one of those grunting sounds when he picked the big ice chest up in his arms. "Grab those two sacks of groceries." He jerked his head at the sacks on the ground. "You help us put stuff away. Maybe Gary'll be home by then."

Brian grabbed the sacks and followed Dad up the steps. When they got to the top, Mama was there to open the door. Brian paused for just a moment. There was still no sign of Gary.

Since Brian had met Gary Marler, they'd been the best of friends. The one thing Brian always did when he and his family arrived at their cabin in Medicine Park was whistle so Gary would know they were there. They stayed together from the first minute Brian arrived until he got in the car for the drive back home to Chickasha.

"Come on, Brian." Mama's voice brought his eyes away from Gary's house and hurried him into the cabin.

It looked just the same as they had left it last summer. There was a lot more dust, but as soon as Brian and Dad finished dragging stuff up from the car, Mama would take care of the dusting and cleaning and all the other things that needed doing.

The front porch was screened in, with thick plastic shutters that were closed to keep the rain and cold out. From the door, the porch went clear across the front of the cabin and around one side. That's where the beds were.

Brian followed Mama through the door on the right where the kitchen and living room were. He put the sacks down next to the ice chest.

"I can't figure it out," Brian complained. "Gary knew we were coming down. He's always here when he knows we're coming. He wouldn't be out playing football when he knew we were gonna be here this afternoon."

Dad came in from the back part of the cabin. Back where the bathroom and the fuse box for the electricity were. He put a hand on Brian's shoulder.

"He might have had to go up to his grandfather's house. The funeral was two weeks ago. He might be up there helping his mom and dad put his belongings together." Dad shrugged. "You know—stuff like that has to be done."

Brian looked up at his dad. There was kind of a heavy feeling in his chest. "Easter vacation is gonna be different, this year. Isn't it, Dad?"

Dad nodded. "You and Gary spent a lot of time with his grampa. And you're right, it is gonna be different—a lot different—without him." Dad's throat bulged out when he swallowed. "You and Gary will be all right, though. You're best friends. Now, he's probably gonna still be feeling sad. You're just gonna have to be patient and understanding with him."

Brian tried to smile. "I'm still feeling kinda sad, too."

Dad put a hand on top of Brian's head and ruffled his hair. "I know. Come on. We got a couple more loads to carry up from the car."

By the time they finished carrying stuff up from the car, Mama was already busy dusting. She'd opened the plastic shutters on the porch to let things air out. Dad got the vacuum sweeper and started to work on the carpet.

Brian went back to the front door. "I'm gonna walk up to Grampa's and see if I can find Gary," he called.

Nobody heard him.

He waved his arms a couple of times. Finally, Dad looked up from his sweeping. Brian motioned to the door. Dad nodded, saying it was okay. Brian stopped on the top step for a moment.

Coming to Medicine Park was like coming to a different world. Back home in Chickasha the land was flat and smooth. There was nothing but rolling hills and a few trees to break up the Oklahoma prairie. But here, at the edge of the Wichita Mountains—only fifty miles from home—it was altogether different.

Medicine Park was in a small valley, nestled between the high mountains all around. The houses were built out of round granite rocks called cobblestones. They were perched against the side of the hills—all facing the river that flowed through the middle of the valley.

It really wasn't a river; it was called Medicine Creek. It wasn't like most of the other rivers Brian had seen in Oklahoma. It wasn't red and muddy-looking. Medicine Creek was a blue color—so clear you could see clean to the bottom in most places.

You had to hunt to find dirt, too. And when you did find dirt, it wasn't red dirt, like around home. Here, it was brown and sandy, washed down from the stone and granite boulders that sprung up from everywhere against the sides of the Wichitas.

It was a beautiful place, wild and rugged. There were areas so hard to get to that, no more than a mile away from the cabin, Brian bet he and Gary could find places no one had ever explored before.

"Brian. Hey, Brian . . . "

Brian blinked. The whispered sound of his name snapped him out of his daydreams. He looked around.

"Brian." The shushed whisper came again. "Brian. Down here."

He looked toward the bottom of the steps. There, on the ground, he spotted the toe of a grungy old tennis shoe. It was so dirty, it was almost brown. The rest of the shoe was hidden behind the pear tree in front of the house.

Brian jumped down the steps. Sure enough, Gary was attached to the other end of the shoe.

"Hey, Gary! What you doing sneaking around and hiding behind that old tree?"

Gary put a finger to his lips. Shushed him.

"I got something to show you, but we can't let nobody else know. Come on."

Brian followed his friend. They moved silently along the wall in front of the cabin. Gary crouched down and went beside the honeysuckle hedge between Brian's cabin and the house to the west. They cut through the backyard of that house, then followed the thick cover of oak trees around the ridge and went back down toward the schoolhouse.

At the edge of the road, Gary crouched down

and looked to make sure there were no cars. Brian squatted beside him, tapping him on the shoulder.

"I'm awful sorry about Grampa's accident."

Gary's eyes were tight when he looked up. His jaw stuck way out, almost mean and determined-looking.

"It was no fishing accident, like everybody thinks," Gary almost growled instead of whispering.

Brian frowned. "Huh?"

"Somebody killed him. I don't know who yet, but I know somebody murdered my grampa. Come on. I'll show you."

CHAPTER 2

There was a little red bridge around back of the school. Brian followed Gary across it. On the other side, they squeezed between the end of the bridge and the brick incinerator where the janitor burned the trash. They moved beside the stream that flowed under the bridge until they came to the place where the rock banks dropped off sharply.

They could hear water bubbling and churning its way through the narrow gorge the stream had cut. Turning sideways, they followed the creek. They squeezed and climbed their way down an almost straight drop to their "private place" at the bottom of the steep canyon.

The Pit is what they called it. It was a small pool of water. A sheer rock cliff surrounded it, like a horseshoe. The top of the cliff was a good twelve feet above their heads, and the walls were smooth and slick as could be. The little stream that had cut it from the solid stone was so small, it didn't have a name. Sometimes, during the dry summer, it slowed down to just a trickle. But the Pit never dried up. Because of the sandbar on the other side.

The stream came from some place up in one of the mountains and flowed into Medicine Creek. Over the years, the stream had piled up chunks of rock and sand and gravel between the Pit and the river. It was kind of like a natural dam that separated them. When the stream stopped flowing, the water from Medicine Creek would seep back through the sand and rock and keep the Pit full of fresh, clean water.

There were cattails growing on the far side of the sandbar. They were so thick that nobody on the other bank or even in a boat out in the middle of the river could see in. About the only way in was through the steep gorge where the boys had just come from. Even then, you had to be a good rock climber to work your way down the gorge and into the Pit. It wasn't an easy place to get to.

Near the bottom, Gary made his way around the edge of the horseshoe to the sandbar. Brian followed him, clinging to the rock wall like a fly until the dry ground was under him.

Even when they were safe on the sandbar, Gary's nervous eyes scanned the ridge above them. Tight, cautious eyes—eyes searching for the slightest movement, the slightest sign that someone might be spying on them.

Brian lay on his stomach. The sandbar was low enough to be shielded from the bite of the brisk spring breeze. The bright sun had warmed the sand. It felt good against Brian's bare arms.

It took a long time for Gary to get settled, to finally satisfy himself that there was no one else around. While Brian waited, Gary kicked his grungy tennis shoes off. Dug his toes down into the hot sand.

At last, he eased over next to Brian and pulled a crumpled yellow envelope from his pocket. The paper was brittle—cracked and colored with age. Inside the envelope was a thin white sheet of paper with lines and a big X on it.

Gary handled it as he would the wings of a butterfly. "It's rice paper," he whispered as he unfolded it. "If you ain't careful, it'll tear."

He spread it out on the sand for Brian to look at. There were lines—marking a trail. On one side, there were some jagged lines, like the peaks of a mountain. And right in the middle was the big X.

"This is the map overlay that shows where the Snake Dancer's Gold is," he said.

He closed the paper carefully and quickly stuck it back in the envelope. Then he pulled out two more pieces of paper.

"This is the note Grampa left. It tells all about

10

the map and how to use the overlay. Grampa left them for us. See, our names are on the outside of the envelope."

Brian scooted closer. He held his breath, listening with excitement. He'd heard Grampa's story about the Snake Dancer's Gold before. But he'd always thought it was just a story. A make-believe kind of story that Grampa told them on days when the weather was bad and they couldn't go outside.

Gary paused. He frowned as he noticed the look on Brian's face. "I never figured it was a real story, either," he confessed. "But this letter Grampa left says different. Listen."

Brian followed along while Gary read. Grampa's handwriting wasn't too good, so his friend did a lot of frowning and head scratching, trying to figure what the words said.

Gary read in a soft voice. Every now and then, he'd stop and look up at the ridge of rock above them—like he was still checking to make sure nobody was watching.

As Brian listened, it was almost like Grampa was there with them. Like it was him telling the story, just as he had so many, many times before.

It coulda been as far back as the start of the Civil War. But to the best of my recollection—the way I heard the story—it was more like the time old Fort Sill was opening up and

11

when the first railhead come to a little town called Rush Springs.

Anyhows, the exact time it all happened ain't all that important. Some of the facts has got sorta messed up, what with the passin' of time and all, but there's one fact for sure. A shipment of gold coin was stolen from a wagon some place between the railhead at Rush Springs and the army base at Fort Sill. I looked it up in some of the old records and the missing gold shipment was writ down.

Nobody knows exactly how much was on the wagon. Somehow the shipments had got all messed up. There was six months' pay for the soldiers at the fort. I've figured it out more than once—and near as I can come, there must have been somewhere in the neighborhood of a million dollars of gold on that wagon.

I first heard the story about the gold when I was ten. Me and a friend named Chancy Becker snuck down to the Indian meeting grounds and crawled up behind the big meeting tepee. (I know I've told you and Brian about the meeting grounds. They used to be on the ball diamond behind the Medicine Park school. Remember the time we went and found them arrowheads?)

Brian closed his eyes. He could almost see Gary and Grampa and him digging around the middle of the ball diamond with their shovels. He hadn't really believed Grampa when he'd told them Indians used to have their powwows there. But after they dug around a time, they found an arrowhead. Brian started believing then. With a shrug of his shoulders he chased the memories out of his head and turned back to listen to the rest of Grampa's story.

The Indians got a good way of remembering things. Instead of writing stuff down and taking a chance on getting it lost, they tell it to others. If anything big was going, everybody what heard the story remembered it and told somebody else. Hunters and warriors told other hunters and warriors they ran into on the trails. Squaws told squaws and braves. Grandmothers passed it down to their children and grandkids around camp fires in front of their tepees. The words and the exact things what happen gets changed around some, but it's remembered. Remembered for a long, long time. It's called a legend. The way I heard it, when I was young, went something like this:

"When again life comes, the Brothers of the Snake go to the secret place in the mountains. Some who have not seen many summers have never visited the place—for they can only go when the waters fall strong and the land floods. It is at this time that the secret place bursts forth and water sprays from the mountain. At this time, and only at this time, may the Brothers of the Snake visit the secret place."

The old medicine man who told the story that night in the tepee said few know the place, for there are few who can call themselves Brother. These few take the others there to dance and make their magic. They talk with the evil spirits—the spirits of darkness, death, and pain.

But the spirits are evil. They do not listen. Instead, they spread their evil to all who come. Many of the Brothers never leave the place.

When the dancing and making of magic is done, the ones who live chase the evil spirits into the mountain. Then, they stop the waters from pouring and lock the spirits away so their evil cannot spread to others of the tribes.

Brian tugged at Gary's arm. Gary paused and looked up at him.

"What?"

Brian frowned. "I don't understand all that stuff."

"What stuff?"

"About the evil spirits and the Indians chasing them back into the mountain. What does it mean?"

Gary rattled the note in his hand. "Grampa explains some of it later on. Just listen, will you?"

With a shrug, Brian nodded, turning his attention back to Grampa's letter.

It was at a time such as this—a time just before the waters burst from the mountain—that the white men discovered the secret cave.

As the Brothers drew near the ending of their ceremony, the white men came to hide the stolen gold. Many of the Brothers were lying dead from their fight with the evil ones. They had come to make war with the evil spirits—not the white man's rifles. Most were weak, ready to give their last strength to drive the evil spirits back into the mountain.

Without warning, the white men swooped in and killed the ones who remained. Killed all, save one.

Hisstoska—Shaman of the Apache—Brother of the Snake—with a bullet near his heart, he alone clung to life.

Wounded and dying, he lay quiet, as though life had already departed for the spirit world. He watched as the whites carried sack after sack of gold into the mountain. Then they left. But in a short time, they returned with more sacks.

Hisstoska heard that they would leave and return once more with the last of their stolen gold. There, they would hide it until they could safely return. They knew nothing of the evil spirits who lived within the mountain, and Hisstoska knew their greed would not let them stay away long before they returned.

He knew also that time was not long for the Brothers of the Snake. Already, many of the evil ones had escaped the mountain. If the others were not driven back and the mountain closed, soon the evil would spread through all the land. Pain and death would come to many. He also knew that if the whites, in their ignorance, were to open the place again, nothing could stop the evil. The Brothers of the Snake were no more. There would be no one to drive the evil back where it lived.

When the whites returned the last time, Hisstoska followed them into the mountain. Many say his magic was strongest of all the shamans. With this great magic, he caused the earth to tremble—the mountain to close. The evil spirits were again locked in their mountain home. So were the white men and their cursed gold. So also was Hisstoska.

The brave deed of Hisstoska took the courage of a spirit—not a man. It is true, some say Hisstoska was a spirit—a soul not of this life. Even the Brothers of the Snake fear the evil which dwells within the mountain. When Hisstoska gave his life to seal the evil inside, he had to seal himself inside also. Close out the light, there to die—alone—with the evil spirits all around, the evil of the white man and the evil that comes of the white man's gold, and the evil that dwells inside the mountain.

Me and Chancy Becker were just a couple of kids when we heard the old Indians telling the story. We was getting a little scared what with the spooky story the old medicine man was telling. We was also thinking about what them Indians might do to us if they was to catch us spying on their private meeting. We was just fixing to sneak off from underneath the tepee when we heard the last part of the story—the part about the curse. The medicine man's eyes got real big and funny-looking when he told that part.

"It is said that before Hisstoska died, he summoned all his magic and brought forth a curse on the white man and his gold. A curse on all who might find it and try to take it from the sacred place. A curse on all who might live now, and who are not now born—that if they open the mountain and release the evil spirits, they shall die. Die a slow and painful death. A curse on all that is within the mountain and death to anyone who takes so much as one coin, one rifle, one arrow from it. And a curse on any Indian who breathes the name Hisstoska before the ears of a white man— for the white man's greed would not allow him to believe the legend, and he would search out the evil. The name Hisstoska is to be spoken of only by the Indian—from now until time is no more.''

Right about then, me and Chancy Becker got to feeling the chills running up and down our backs. We lit out of there in a hurry, figuring the Indians were liable to see us any second. But we heard the story about the Curse of the Snake Dancer's Gold. We heard the story and we never forgot it.

It had taken Gary a long time to read Grampa's story. Brian had been sitting very still. Now he noticed his back was hurting a bit from being so stiff. His elbows were getting raw from propping them under his head in the sand. He stretched and got to his feet.

"I remember Grampa telling us the story," Brian said. "Once, when we were studying about Indians in school, I told my teacher about the legend."

"And?" Gary urged him on.

"And my teacher said that only the Navajo and the Hopi Indians did that snake dancing stuff. She said that they never lived in Oklahoma—not even when it was mostly an Indian reservation."

Gary smiled. "My teacher said that the Kiowa Indians were the only ones who lived in Oklahoma a long time ago. She said about the same thing your teacher did. I told Grampa about it."

Brian leaned closer. "So what did he say?"

"Grampa says there's a lot the white man *thinks* he knows about the Indians. But there's more that only the Indians know, that they won't never tell about."

"Really?"

"Yep! He said only the shamans or medicine men knew about the secret place. He said there's lots of stuff the Indian tribes keep secret, but there's stuff that the shamans even kept secret from their own tribes—you know, special medicines, things about the spirits, and stuff they didn't even tell the chief about."

Brian felt a tingle at the back of his neck.

"I'm glad Grampa wrote the story down for us," he told Gary. "But what about that other piece of paper? The real thin stuff. What did you say it was?"

"Rice paper."

"Yeah. What's that for?"

There was another piece of paper under the one Grampa had written his story on. Gary unfolded it. Brian frowned.

They had been lying on the sandbar for a long time. Brian didn't like being that still. And he didn't really want to listen to another story.

"What's that?" he asked.

19

Gary held the paper out to him. "It's the rest of Grampa's story. Want to hear it?"

Brian scratched at his nose. "I'm kinda tired of sittin'. Why don't you just tell me what it says?"

"Okay." Gary shrugged.

He stuffed the paper back in his pocket and pulled his shoes on. Then he got up, stretching as Brian had done. Real slow, they started walking toward the narrow gorge that led out of the Pit, back the way they came. Gary paused. He picked up a little rock and tossed it into the pool of water.

"Grampa said in that letter that he had a big black folder with maps in it. He said that he and Chancy Becker decided they'd find the gold and get rich. So every place they looked, they kept a map of it. When they were through searching one spot, they'd mark it off the maps so they wouldn't look there again. He said that about ten years ago, he and Chancy found out that somebody had been following them. So they made two sets of maps and split up. That way, whoever was watching them couldn't follow so easy."

Gary pitched another rock at the pool of water, then started up the narrow split in the rock. He talked over his shoulder as he climbed. "He said that he knew for a fact that the curse was true. A fella named McAimly stumbled on the place where the gold was hid, about nine years back. He even brought a handful of it into town, showing it around. But before he could ever get back there for the rest or tell anybody where it was, he got killed by a hit-and-run driver. Eight years ago, Grampa's friend, Chancy Becker, got killed in a hunting accident. Nobody knew who shot him, but when they found him and brought him back to town, there were some gold coins in his pocket. Grampa said that Chancy's wife knew where the gold was, but she was so afraid of the curse, she'd never tell nobody."

Gary groaned as he pulled himself over the top of the cliff. Brian followed him. At the top of the Pit, they both looked around.

"What about that thin piece of paper you showed me?" Brian asked.

"It's an overlay."

"What's that mean?"

"Well . . . " Gary frowned, not knowing quite how to explain. "The paper's so thin, you can see clear through it. Up at the very top, it says 'page 59.' I figure that Grampa found the gold and made that overlay. If we look on page 59 of Grampa's maps and put the overlay on top of it, we'll know exactly where the Snake Dancer's Gold is buried."

Brian felt his eyes bug out. "You mean all that gold—" He broke off because a big knot came up in his throat.

"Yep," Gary answered.

"Well . . . er . . . let's . . . " Brian was stuttering so hard he could barely get the words out. "Let's go get the maps and—"

21

"We can't," Gary cut him off.

Brian frowned. "Why not?"

"They're not there."

"What do you mean, not there?"

Gary shrugged. "Somebody stole 'em."

"Stole 'em!" Brian gasped. "Who? When?"

Gary patted the letter he had folded in his pocket. "Grampa said that he found the gold. He also said that when he was coming down from the mountain, he found tracks, and he knew there had been somebody following him. He said that when he woke up the next morning, he found a tear in the window screen where somebody had tried to break into his room. They got spooked or somethin' and didn't get nothin'. He figured whoever it was was after his maps. So he made that overlay on the rice paper and hid it. Then he marked out the place on the map so if somebody got it, they'd think he'd already looked there and hadn't found anything."

"First off, you say Grampa's maps got stole— then you say nothin' got stole." Brian scratched his head. "Which really happened?"

Gary sneered at him. "Nothing got took the first time. I found this letter, to us, hid in my tackle box. Grampa must have stuck it there the night he died—the night he went fishing. Anyhow, last Monday, about a week after Grampa's funeral, I went with Mom and Dad to gather his stuff up to store in our attic. I was in his room, looking for the black case with the maps. Only when I got there, I found another screen torn up and a different window opened. Outside, I found some tracks in the dirt. Tracks where somebody had crawled in the window. They musta broke in while we were at his funeral. Broke in and stole Grampa's maps."

Brian bit at his bottom lip. "But who? Who coulda done it?"

Gary shrugged. "I don't know who, but I bet whoever it was was the same person who killed Grampa."

Gary's eyes got real tight. The anger turned his face a bright color of red. Brian put his hands on his hips, glaring back at Gary.

"But how do you know that's what really happened? Dad told me that when your dad called to tell us what happened, he explained that Grampa had slipped on the rocks while he was fishing and drowned. Maybe whoever stole the maps didn't have nothin' to do with Grampa's death. Maybe it really was an accident."

Gary shook his head. "It *wasn't!!*"

"You sure?"

"I'm sure."

Brian shrugged. "Everybody else says it was an accident. How can you be so sure it wasn't?"

Gary's eyes got tight again. "First place, Grampa went fishing in that same spot about twice a week. I bet he walked up and down that bank a million times and never slipped once—"

"That don't mean nothing," Brian broke in. "He still coulda slipped this time."

Gary shook his head. "I doubt it. 'Sides, there's some other things, too."

"Like what?"

"Like his stink bait. You know how he always set it right beside him, and never put the top back on the thing?"

Brian felt his nose crinkle up. "I remember."

"Well, when the sheriff called us and said he was missing, we went with a bunch of other folks to search. I found Grampa's stink bait, and the lid was *closed*. Once he started fishing, he never closed the stink bait. Grampa always had three rods out. The Shakespeare was his favorite. He set the other two out on the bank, but he kept the Shakespeare right with him and the stink bait."

Brian nodded. "I remember."

"Well . . . " Gary went on. "When we got there, that new spinning reel Dad got him for Christmas was by the stink bait. The Shakespeare was clear down the bank."

Brian shook his head. "That sure don't sound like Grampa." He stuck a finger in his ear and wiggled it. "But why? Everybody liked Grampa. Nobody would want to hurt *him*. Would they?"

Gary looked down and picked at one of his fingernails.

"If somebody knew about him finding the gold. If they knew about that and wanted the gold all for themselves . . . "

He choked up, breaking off what he was saying.

Brian clenched his fist at his side. "I wish we knew who done it," he growled. "I'd give anything if we could find out who killed Grampa. Why don't you tell Mr. Ralston, the sheriff, about the letter?"

Gary shook his head. "No."

"But why not?"

"No," he repeated. "I ain't even told Mom and Dad. It's something we got to do by ourselves. Grampa left *us* that letter. It wasn't meant for anybody else—just you and me. We got to find out who done it."

"How?"

Gary frowned. "I don't rightly know, but I think I found a track. It was in the sand by the road near Grampa's fishing spot."

"What kind of track?"

"Car track. There was a cut in one of the right tires, like it'd run over a piece of broken glass. I showed it to Sheriff Ralston. He said it might be important and he'd make a plaster cast of it. I figure if we find a car that's got a chunk out of its tire like that one, we'll find who killed Grampa."

For some reason, they stopped talking and looked around. Neither had been paying much attention to where they were going. When they stopped, they were standing in front of Brian's cabin.

Right about then, Brian heard his stomach

growl. He slapped a hand over it. The way he had things figured, it was going to take a lot of walking and hunting to find that car with the cut wheel. Walking and hunting was a lot of hard work, especially on an empty stomach.

"You want to come up and eat dinner with us?" he asked.

Gary shielded his eyes, looking up at the bright sun. "We done missed dinner. It's about four o'clock."

Brian's stomach made another grumbling sound. "Great." Then he shrugged. "Well, we might as well start looking at car tires."

Gary nodded.

"Might as well."

They spent that afternoon until dark and the next two days looking at almost every car tire in the whole town of Medicine Park.

The first day, nothing happened at all. On the second day, some old man saw them looking at his car and came running out yelling something about thieving kids stealing his gas.

After the man accused them of stealing gas and ran them off, they started taking turns. One would check the tires and the other would stand watch. Gary squatted down under the fender of a green pickup. All of a sudden, Brian saw this little bitty white poodle come racing around the corner of the house.

He opened his mouth to warn Gary, but he

didn't even have time to get the words out. That little poodle raced right behind Gary, reached up, and bit him on the bottom, then took off around the house again.

Gary yelled and jumped up. Only when he jumped up, he was still under the fender of that green pickup, so he clunked himself on the head good and solid.

Gary rubbed his bottom with one hand and his head with the other. He glared at Brian with a mean look in his eye. "Some friend you are," he growled. "You're supposed to be standing guard."

Brian held his hands out helplessly. "I didn't have time. I opened my mouth to yell at you, but the dog was so quick, he done had your bottom bit before any words could come out."

Gary kept rubbing his bottom with one hand and his head with the other. Brian got tickled, watching him. He had to bite his lips together to keep from laughing. Gary was trying to glare at him, but he got tickled, too.

"Ain't funny." He tried to sound mean, only he started chuckling.

They were just up the road from the gas station. They headed back, and when they got there, Brian followed Gary into the bathroom. Once inside, Gary dropped his jeans and tried to look back over his shoulder to see how much damage the little poodle had done.

"Don't think it broke the skin, did it?"

Brian frowned. "Nope. Just bruised."

Gary pulled his pants up. "Sure do smart."

He rubbed at his bottom a few more times, then they headed off to check some more cars.

Brian had to check the next five in a row, while Gary stood watch. After that, they started taking turns again. Only every time Gary bent down to look at a tire, he looked around real careful to make sure there weren't any dogs around. He kept one hand down across his backside—making sure his bottom was protected.

It was about an hour or so before dark when they finally decided to give it up.

"We've looked at most every tire in Medicine Park and still haven't found a clue," Gary said.

Brian nodded. "Reckon we could spend the rest of our lives looking at car tires and never find a thing. Besides, my back's getting sore from all this bending over."

"Mine, too," Gary admitted. Only Brian noticed he was rubbing his bottom where the dog bit him instead of his back.

"I'm getting kinda hungry," Brian said. "Why don't we run back by the house and see if there's anything around to eat?"

Gary reached down in his pocket. "Hey, I got some money. Why don't we go to Ralston's store and get a pop and some peanuts or somethin'? After that, we can go down to the Arcade."

"What's the Arcade?"

"It's a new place they put in that little shop

next to the Ole Plantation. Got some brand-new video games—then they got Pac-Man and Frogger and all them other old ones that are fun. Anyhow, I got a few quarters. While we're playing the games, we can be figuring out a plan for what to do next. This looking at car tires ain't working. We got to figure another plan for catchin' Grampa's murderer.''

CHAPTER 3

Along with being the sheriff, Odie Ralston also ran the store on the other side of the creek. Mostly, he ran the store, because there wasn't much for him to do as sheriff in a little town like Medicine Park. Every now and then he'd catch a speeder. And sometimes he'd run up to the Carter place and stop a fight. But that was only when Mr. and Mrs. Carter got to yelling and screaming at each other so loud the neighbors couldn't sleep.

Odie greeted the boys with his loud, ugly laugh—a laugh that seemed to say he was only pretending to be friendly and good-natured, when all along he really wasn't. He rocked back on his heels behind the counter and let his fat stomach poke out.

"Howdy, boys," he blabbered. "Come on in. Ain't seen you in a coon's age."

Brian gave a half-smile. "Hello, Mr. Ralston. How are you today?"

"Mr. Ralston . . . " Gary pushed his way in front of Brian. "Have you been able to find that car with the cut tire?"

Odie's broad smile disappeared as the corners of his mouth drooped. He scratched thoughtfully at his chin, only he didn't have much chin to scratch. It sort of sank into his face, like his chin was so small it looked almost like part of his neck. Finally, he shook his head.

"No, Gary, I haven't." Then, with that fake smile, he added, "But I ain't through looking. I'll keep on looking long as I got the strength in me."

Brian felt his eyes roll back into the top of his head. He'd heard a lot of windbags before, but Odie Ralston had to be the windiest. Brian bet he'd no more been looking for that car than a cat would go looking for a dog. It was against his nature to do *anything* that took work. He'd probably been sitting around his store all day.

Odie had been hacking at some beefsteak with a big cleaver on a chopping block. And his apron was all splattered with blood and grease.

"What brings you boys over here?"

Brian noticed Gary digging in his pocket.

"Thought we'd get us somethin' to eat. Will this pay for two pops and two candy bars?"

He put some change on the counter. Odie snatched it up just about the time it hit.

He frowned. "Nope," he answered.

Gary dug into his pocket again. "How much more?"

"Nickel."

Odie snatched the nickel from Gary's hand before he had a chance to lay it down. Then he trotted off to the front of the store. In a second or two, Brian heard the cash register jingle. He could hear Odie humming a tune to himself.

Gary leaned close to Brian's ear. "That Odie likes his money almost as much as he likes his food."

Gary stuck his stomach out real big, like Odie's. Brian had to bite down on his lip to keep from laughing out loud. Quickly, he turned and headed to the other side of the store where the pop machine was . . . and where Odie wouldn't see him laughing.

He fished two cold pops out of the ice water in the bottom of the machine for him and Gary. Then he walked back to the front of the store where Gary was standing by the candy counter.

"What'll it be?" Odie slid open the glass drawer.

"I'll have a Snickers." Gary pointed.

"Brian?"

"Same, please, Mr. Ralston."

Odie handed them the candy bars, then he sat

down in a big, overstuffed chair behind the counter.

Brian and Gary both thanked him and started for the door.

"Hold up a minute, boys," Odie called.

Brian opened the door. Paused. "Yes sir?"

Odie moaned as he lifted his fat body out of the chair.

"You ain't plannin' to take them there cans, are you?"

Brian looked at the can in his hand. Shrugged. Beside him, he could hear Gary munching on his candy bar.

"We'll be coming back tomorrow, Odie. Figured we'd bring 'em back to you then." He had a mouthful of candy and it was a mite hard to understand him.

Odie's fat jowls dropped when he frowned. "I know you boys got good intentions. But you might forget. Or you might accidentally drop them there cans. Them things cost me money, you know. You boys got to either pay for 'em or leave 'em here."

Brian glanced down into his can. It was still over half full. Gary nudged him with an elbow.

" 'Bout finished?"

Brian shrugged. "Reckon I can," he said, taking a deep swig. It burned his nose when he tried to drink so fast. His eyes started to water. "Figure it's gonna take me a couple of minutes, though."

Gary nodded. "That's all right. It'll give me time to finish mine." Then, turning so he could speak loud enough for Odie to hear, he added, "I'd sure hate to forget and take my candy wrapper with me. Make me feel like I was cheatin' somebody."

Odie frowned. "Ain't no sense gettin' smart aleck, Gary. I'm just doin' what I got to. If I was to let every kid in Medicine Park take their can out of here . . . why, I wouldn't make no money at all when I take a load of cans to the recycling place in Lawton."

Gary ducked his head sheepishly.

"Sorry, Mr. Ralston. I didn't mean to be smart with you."

Brian took another drink of his pop. It sure wasn't much fun trying to drink it fast, but he was ready to leave.

After a time, Odie quit staring at them. He moved toward the back of the store, counting boxes and jotting stuff down on a piece of paper.

"When you boys finish," he called, "just put the cans in the box. I'll trust you."

"Trust us," Gary whispered. "He trusts us about as much as a chicken trusts a hungry coyote. Bet he don't take them beady eyes off us till we leave."

Brian took another long drink. The bubbles hit his nose. Made him shake his head.

"He is a mite tight," Brian agreed.

Gary made a snorting sound when he tried to hold his laugh in. "I always thought he wore his pants too tight," he snickered. "Only them pants ain't near as tight as he is."

They finished most of the pop and put the cans in the box. They made sure to rattle them around some, so Odie would know they had done what he asked.

They had gone about a block down the hill from Odie's store when Brian turned and looked back with a frown.

"I know you don't care much for Odie," he said. "I don't neither, to be real honest with you. But . . ."

"What you trying to say?" Gary urged.

"Well . . ." Brian swallowed. "He is the sheriff. I mean, maybe if we was to show him Grampa's note . . . maybe it'd help him find who killed Grampa."

Gary shook his head one last time. Then he turned and started up the road.

"Nope. It ain't a bad idea, but there's something else I want to try first."

Brian trotted after him. "What?"

Gary kept walking. Without looking back, he answered, "The Becker place."

Brian froze in his tracks. He stood there, his mouth gaping open, and watched Gary moving off. Finally, he chased after him.

"Gary," he called. "Wait up."

Gary kept right on walking. Brian finally caught up to him. He grabbed his arm. Spun him around.

"You don't mean that crazy lady what lives up on the hill?"

Gary nodded. "That's her. Remember, in Grampa's note it said she was the only living person who knew where the Snake Dancer's Gold was hid. If we can get her to tell us where it is, we can go there and wait for whoever stole Grampa's maps to come looking around. Then we'll know who stole them maps."

Gary turned and pulled his arm away. "Come on."

Brian hesitated. "I don't know, Gary . . . it's gettin' mighty late . . . and . . . "

"Ah, come on. You ain't scared, are you?" Gary smiled.

Brian stuck his chin out. "No. I ain't scared. It's only . . . only . . . "

"Ah, shucks." Gary laughed. "Them stories about her is probably nothin' but rumors. I bet she ain't really a witch. And if her old house really was haunted, she wouldn't be living there, would she? And them stories about her carrying an ax around all the time so she can chop people's heads off and cook 'em in that big black kettle—I bet them is just wild stories somebody dreamed up. Come on. It won't hurt none to just go up there and look around."

Brian stopped dead in his tracks.

Ever since his family had first started coming to the cabin at Medicine Park, he had heard stories about the crazy old witch who lived on Rattlesnake Hill. Strange, eerie stories that made the hair stand up on the back of his neck. Stories that he remembered when he was walking alone at night. Stories that made him listen—turn and watch for something following him in the dark.

Mrs. Becker's was one of the few places in Medicine Park that he and Gary hadn't gone to before. Somehow, they always managed to stay clear of the spooky old house.

Only Gary wasn't leaving him much choice. He was bound and determined to go. And if Brian wanted to be with his friend, he'd have to go, too.

Brian's knees were shaking. But he swallowed and took a deep breath. Then he trotted off after Gary.

CHAPTER 4

Halfway up the side of Rattlesnake Hill, the road came to a dead-end. A small, winding path led from there to the top of the hill.

Gary stopped. His feet didn't move as he stood—stood frozen, staring at something up ahead.

"There!" Gary's voice was a whisper. Tight. Nervous. "That's it! That's the Becker place."

Brian felt a lump in his throat. He could see a house through some trees ahead. It seemed out of place. Lonely. Like something that was once real nice but had long been forgotten and left to age and decay. It was deserted, scary. Instead of the house being made of cobblestone, like the rest of the houses in Medicine Park, it was all wood, brown and cracked-looking. There were gobs of trees and bushes, crowded up against it, smothering it with green, tangled vines. Ivy and spring creeper had crawled up the side of the house and wrapped themselves in a solid mat, gnarled and tangled, around the rock chimney.

The way the door and the two upstairs windows set, it made the front of the house look like a face. The two windows were eyes, the door a puckered-up mouth.

The old house would have been scary enough at high noon. But to Brian, standing in the half shadows of an Oklahoma sunset, it was like seeing a haunted castle straight out of a picture show.

Gary motioned Brian to follow him as he moved up the hill. It was starting to get dark. The dim, shifting shadows made it hard to see. The closer they got to the Becker house, the more Brian wanted to turn around and go back home. He tugged at Gary's sleeve.

"Let's wait till tomorrow," he whispered.

"No."

"That way, it'll be light enough to see good," he argued. "When it's good and light—"

"No," Gary cut him off.

"But we could come back early, and—"

"No!"

"But . . . Gary . . . "

"Come on. It won't take long, Brian."

Brian held his arm, making him stop.

Gary turned with an irritated frown.

"What's wrong? You scared?"

Brian glared back at him. "No, I ain't scared," he lied. "It's only . . . well . . . "

"Look," Gary snapped. "If you're scared to go with me, stay here. Go on home, if you want. But me, I'm going up and have me a look-see. I'm gonna talk to that Mrs. Becker."

Gary yanked his arm away and marched on toward the spooky-looking house. Brian hesitated, but only for a second. He was soon following right behind his friend. Moving on quiet feet. Holding his breath.

The trees grew thicker as they neared the old house. When they moved through them, the darkness seemed to close in. And it was quiet. So quiet that Brian could almost hear his heart thumping in his ears. Around this time of evening, the wind usually settled. Without the push of the wind, the leaves didn't rattle on the trees and the limbs didn't shake and squeak. It was usually quiet this time of day, only Brian couldn't ever remember it being *this* quiet.

He reached up and tugged at Gary's arm again. Gary jumped and wheeled around. "Don't do that," he whispered. "It's spooky enough round here without you grabbin' me."

Brian motioned with his head for Gary to lean close to him. "I got a bad feelin'," Brian confessed. "I got a bad feelin' about this place."

"It's just your imagination." Gary looked around all nervous-like. "It'll only take us a minute. We'll look in the barn and then the shed, then get out of here.''

Brian bit at his bottom lip.

"I . . . I figure we're gonna get in trouble. We're already late for supper, and . . . if this old lady's really crazy, like everybody says . . . hard tellin' what she's liable to do. Come on. Let's go home.''

Gary swayed back and forth from one foot to the other like he was having trouble making up his mind. Finally, he shook his head.

"No. We're already here. We won't ask her about the maps. I just want to look at her. See if she really is crazy. She won't even know we been around.''

Gary led the way toward the rickety old woodshed. They stayed at the edge of the trees, using the long shadows and the brush as cover so they couldn't be seen.

The house seemed empty. There were no lights. No sounds coming from the open front door. Through the vines and stuff, the boys could see some of the windows. They stopped to look inside, just to make sure there was no one stirring there, then moved on again.

The old shed and a barn were about fifty yards from the house. When they came up from the trees, the shed was closer. When they got to the edge of it, Gary suddenly jerked and stopped dead in his tracks.

"What is it?" Brian urged.

Gary shushed him. "Listen."

There was a sound. An unfamiliar, far-off sound. Brian frowned, tilting his head to the side, trying to hear what it was. Although he couldn't hear it well, the sound reminded him of some kind of machine. A grinding, buzzing sound, sort of like the electric sander Dad had in his workroom back home. Only it was different. It was slower than a machine. Much slower.

"What is it?" Brian whispered.

Gary shrugged. "Don't know. Sounds like it's coming from the barn."

"Let's get outa here," Brian urged.

Gary shook his head. "No. Listen."

The sound had stopped. Brian sighed. He didn't know what had been making that strange sound, but he was glad it stopped.

Gary motioned him to follow. They moved around the edge of the rickety woodshed to where the door was. Brian saw Gary's hand shake as it reached out for the door handle.

The rusty old hinges squeaked as the door swung open. Brian leaned around. He squinted, trying to see into the darkness of the shed.

He couldn't see anything—not at first. But after a few seconds of staring into the darkness, his eyes got used to it. In the back of the shed were some wood risers and some boxes with straw in them. Judging from the smell of the place, it had to have been a chicken coop at one time. But there was other stuff there, too. Old tools and boxes filled with scraps of junk. Hanging from the walls, Brian could make out leather harnesses, the kind they used on plow horses in the old days. There was a saddle covered with dust, and some ropes that looked dry enough to crack in two if anybody were to try and use them. Ropes that were too big for lassos. Ropes that hung from the rafters with cobwebs woven in between them, making them look like drapes or curtains.

There was gobs and gobs of stuff in the little shed, so much stuff that it would be hard for anyone to get inside the place, much less walk around.

Brian felt his shoulders slump. He sighed, relieved that they hadn't found Old Lady Becker.

The door squeaked again when Gary closed it. But along with the squeaking sound of the door, there was another sound.

"What are you boys doin' in my shed?"

The angry, high-pitched voice screeched close beside them. Brian jumped so hard his stomach bounced clear up to his throat. He almost fell when he wheeled around to see who was there.

Only a few feet away, a form took shape in the doorway of the big barn. It came from the shadows, inside. Came from the darkness into the dim light that seemed to move and change shape with the flickering movement of the tree limbs.

Brian froze. He could feel the tingle run up and down his back. Feel the hair stand up straight on the back of his neck.

It was a witch!

"What are you boys doin' in my shed?" the crackly voice demanded again.

Brian could see her plainly now. He took a step back and froze, trembling.

She was small and withered with age. Her long black dress made her hard to see when she came from the darkness. Her face was wrinkled and drawn. Her eyes were dark black, like the night. Long white hair spun and twisted its way clear down past her shoulders—wild-looking hair that stood out in all directions. And in her hands—in her wrinkled, twisted hands—she carried an ax.

The sun had gone behind the mountains, but a round, full moon had come up to replace a little of its light. The white light of the moon caught the blade. Light reflected from the ax so brightly that it was almost like a mirror.

Brian's throat was tight. He couldn't swallow. Gary held to the door of the shed like he was stuck.

"You boys get away from there," her gravel-like voice roared sharp. "Get!—'Fore I skin ya alive."

She came toward them. The light glistened from the sharp blade of the ax as she came nearer.

CHAPTER 5

Brian never ran so hard or so fast or so scared in his life.

He was over halfway down the hill before he thought to look and see if Gary had got away from that old witch with her ax. He paused to look back.

Gary was right at his heels. He was moving on like a runaway freight train headed down a mountain. He shot past, wasn't about to stop for anything!

Brian started in after him.

"Wait up!"

Only Gary wasn't waiting on nobody. Brian took off, running until he was right beside Gary. They didn't break stride and slow to a walk until they reached the driveway in front of Gary's house. They were out of breath, wheezing and gasping for air.

"Was . . . that . . . her?" Brian puffed.

Gary nodded his head. Brian leaned against the cobblestone wall around Gary's front yard. Gary turned and boosted himself up on one of the stones.

"Don't look like nobody's home," he sighed. "Must be over to your house."

Brian climbed up the wall to sit beside him. The dew had already started to settle on the long stems of grass. Feeling the wet, he leaned to the side and felt his seat. Then he smiled, knowing it wasn't wet enough to matter.

Gary coughed and took a deep breath. "That was Mrs. Becker," he puffed. "I heard some of the older guys at school saying she was a real witch, only I never believed them." He blew his breath up his forehead. Shook his hair to the side. "I believe 'em now, though."

Brian nodded, agreeing. "Did ya see her hair? And that ax!" He shuddered, just remembering. "What you reckon she was plannin' to do to us?"

"Chop us up into little pieces." There was a loud gulping sound from Gary's throat when he answered. "But that ain't gonna stop me. She knows about the Snake Dancer's Cave and the gold. And whoever stole Grampa's maps is looking for that gold. If we can get her to tell us where it is, we can be there waiting whenever Grampa's killer shows up. We can be there to catch him red-handed." He sighed, wiping the sweat from his forehead. "She just startled us tonight. Tomorrow, when it's light, we'll go back. We won't let her scare us off this time. We'll go back and make her talk to us."

Brian felt his eyes roll back. For a minute, Gary had seemed as scared as he was. Now he was talking about sneaking back to that spooky old place. Going back up on Rattlesnake Hill to talk with that crazy old witch who came swinging the shiny ax at them. Brian felt his mouth curl up on the side, as he looked at his friend.

"You're as crazy as that old lady, you know that, Gary?"

Gary frowned. "Huh?"

"You're crazy. You'd have to be nuts to go back there."

"But she knows about the Snake Dancer's Gold. We got to talk to her. Got to find out—"

"She ain't about to talk to us. She'd just as soon chop us up in little pieces. What we ought to do is tell Odie Ralston. He'd know what to do with that letter Grampa left us. He'd know how to talk to Mrs. Becker. Let's go tell him."

Gary frowned. He tilted his head to the side, thinking.

"I don't know, Brian. . . . I don't think Grampa wanted us to tell nobody about that letter. Besides, Odie's kind of a stingy old creep. I don't trust him."

Brian nodded.

"I don't trust him, neither, Gary. I don't even like him. But he is the sheriff. It's his job. He's hired to find clues and stuff. And like you said, that letter must be a clue to who killed Grampa. Let's show him."

Gary let his chin droop against his chest. He closed his eyes and sat there a long time, thinking.

"What do you think?" Brian tried to hurry him. "Let's tell him. First thing in the morning."

Gary didn't answer. Brian folded his arms. "I think we ought to tell him," he urged again. "I don't think it's smart to go back and try to talk with Old Lady Becker. That's the dumbest thing you could do. That'd be downright stupid."

Gary eased to his feet. He planted his hands on his hips and glared at Brian. "You callin' me stupid?"

Brian shook his head. "No. I didn't say you was stupid. I said if you went back to that spooky old house, you'd *be* stupid."

"That's the same thing," Gary sneered.

"No, it ain't."

Gary folded his arms and made his lips curl. "You're scared, ain't you? You're sayin' stuff about going to tell Odie 'cause you're scared to go back up there."

Brian frowned. "No, I ain't."

"You are too. You're scared. That's why you

want to go tell the sheriff. You're scared to go back there."

"I ain't," Brian protested.

"Are too," Gary snapped.

"Ain't."

"Are!"

"Ain't!"

"Are!"

"Ain't! AIN'T! *AIN'T!*"

Gary glared down at him. "I never figured my best friend in the whole world was a chicken."

Brian felt his eyes squint up. "You ain't got no right to say stuff like that, Gary."

Gary's nose crinkled up. "I can say it if it's true. And you're a big, fat chicken."

Brian felt his fist clench at his side. Slowly, he got to his feet. "You take that back!"

"Will not. Chicken."

"Gary! I'm warnin' you . . . "

"Chicken!"

"Gary . . . "

"Chicken, chicken, chicken!"

Brian felt the muscles in his arms draw tight. His legs tensed, ready to spring.

"You say that one more time, I'll knock your block off."

"Ha," Gary laughed. "You and who else?"

"I mean it, Gary."

There was a short silence. Then Gary's soft voice: "Chicken."

Brian was all over him. Swinging and hitting. But, it was like Gary was waiting for him, because the second he started swinging and hitting at Gary, Gary started swinging and hitting back.

In a twinkling, though, their anger had brought them so close there wasn't room for swinging and hitting. They were wrapped up in each other. Arms tangled around arms. Hands clutched at fistfuls of hair. And finally, when one of them lost his balance, they both went tumbling. Head over heels, they rolled down the sloping driveway.

Brian felt the gravel bite at his elbow and back as he rolled. That didn't stop him, though. He kept slugging at Gary. Every once in a while, he felt the soft "give" as his knuckles slammed into Gary's stomach.

Then, somehow, things got all messed up. First thing Brian knew, they had stopped rolling. He was lying face down on the gravel at the edge of the road. He tried to get up, but he couldn't. It didn't take long to figure out what was happening, either.

Gary was sitting astride his back, like a cowboy riding a wild bronc. Brian tried to throw him off—only every time he raised his head, Gary'd hit it, making Brian's face bounce against the pavement. It felt like his head was a basketball and Gary was bouncing it up and down on the road. Finally, with every bit of strength he had,

Brian pushed. He twisted and rolled to the side. Gary yelled as he lost his balance.

In a split second, Brian was on top of him. He sat square in the middle of Gary's stomach, his knees planted firm on his shoulders. Now *he* was on top. He started pounding Gary in the face. He'd punch him, then wait till Gary's head had time to bounce against the road before he hit him again.

All of a sudden, Gary shoved, using his legs and arms to lift his back off the ground. Brian felt himself falling. He grabbed for Gary about the same time Gary grabbed for him. Wrapped in each other's arms again, they started wrestling. Pushing and struggling against one another. Grabbing hair and biting—when they got a chance. And with all the pushing and tugging and hair-pulling, they started rolling again.

They kept rolling, over and over each other, until they rolled clean across the road. And when they got to the other side, there was only one place left to go.

There was this gutter that ran alongside the Medicine Park road. It was a pretty wide gutter, but only about six feet deep. Down at the bottom there was a whole bunch of water and . . . well, folks in Medicine Park had been talking for a long time about building sewers. That way, the runoff from the septic tanks wouldn't go into the creek and spoil the water there. Only sewer pipe cost a lot of money, and seeing how folks didn't have much money to spend, they decided to leave things like they were.

The runoff and overflow from all the septic tanks in Medicine Park emptied into that small gutter that followed along the road. The septic tanks from the school, the houses, the café— *everything*—sinks, showers, bathtubs, and even toilets—all emptied into that gutter.

The smell wasn't too bad, not unless you got up close to it in the summertime. Then it'd make your eyes spin in your head and you'd have to hold your nose to keep from gagging.

Brian and Gary kept wrestling and rolling. Then the smell hit them. They tried to stop rolling, only by the time they realized where they were going, it was too late.

The two of them had rolled clean across the road and tumbled down the steep slant at the edge of the gully. Neither one even had time to let go of the other and try to catch himself before they hit the "stuff" at the bottom.

They didn't hit with a splash. It was more like sliding across the slick, slimy mud in a hog pen. It was kind of a gushy, oozy feeling. Then there was a slow sinking.

Brian felt the wet ooze all around. He clamped his mouth shut. Made the air rush out his nose. Only that didn't keep him from tumbling clean over the wet, slimy gunk that floated in the bottom of the gully.

Without losing a second, he jumped to his feet. The green, slimy stuff was slippery, but he managed to claw and clamber his way up the bank and back to the road.

Gary came crawling up right behind him. He was wet from head to toe. He raked his fingers through his hair and shook himself like a wet dog just out of a bath.

It was a funny sight, only Brian couldn't laugh. He was afraid to open his mouth. Afraid to even breathe. But sooner or later, he was going to have to. It took all the courage he had to open his mouth and finally draw in a breath of air.

He coughed. Gagged on the horrible smell.

"I think I'm gonna be sick," he moaned.

"Yuck," Gary sputtered. "I already *am*."

Suddenly, the bright lights of a car hit them. It hurt Brian's eyes. He blinked, shielding his eyes from the blinding lights. The car screeched to a stop, just a few feet in front of them. The door squeaked when it swung open.

"What in the devil's going on here?" a deep voice grumbled.

Odie Ralston came into view in front of the headlights.

"Were you two making all that racket over here? I thought there was a couple of tomcats fighting. Never heard such a commotion."

He pointed at the car. "Come on. Get in the car—I'll take you to clean up."

Brian heard his tennis shoes slosh when he

walked. "But Mr. Ralston—" Brian started to argue, but Odie cut him off.

"It's dark. There's folks trying to sleep around here. Now, get in the car."

Brian looked at Gary. Gary looked back at him. They both shrugged and started sloshing toward the car.

All of a sudden, Odie started coughing. Frantically, he waved for them to stop.

"What in the world!?" He choked. "You two smell like . . . like . . . "

"Like the sewer?" Gary asked.

"The sewer?" Odie reeled back toward his car. "You two been in that sewer trench?"

Brian and Gary looked at each other. It was hard to see through all the green slime that dripped from their hair. Gary turned to Mr. Ralston with a shrug.

"It was an accident, sir."

"Yeah," Brian agreed. "We was just sorta playin' around and . . . well . . . we accidentally fell in. We didn't mean to."

Odie Ralston moaned. "Good grief! Get away from my car!"

He made some angry noises and came trotting around the car for a better look at them. He held a hand over his nose, protecting it from the rank smell that reeked from the two soggy adventurers. After looking at them for a long time, he settled back against the hood of his car.

Brian watched him. He could hear Odie mumbling something, only he couldn't make out what he was saying because the water in his ears made it hard to hear. He could hear the water and "stuff" dripping off him. It made a plopping sound when it fell in giant drops to the road. Gary stood beside him, shivering from the cold. He was still coughing and gagging from the smell that gushed up from their clothes.

"I'm gonna die if I don't get this stuff off me pretty soon," he whispered.

Brian nodded. "Me too."

He stood with his arms out away from his sides. He had his face all scrunched up and his mouth closed tight so the stuff that was dripping down off his hair wouldn't get in. It seemed like Odie was going to sit there forever. He kept frowning, like he was working something out. As Brian stood waiting, he couldn't figure out which he disliked the most—being sopping wet and cold at the same time, or smelling like an outhouse.

All of a sudden, Gary let out a yelp. Brian glanced over and saw him leaping and dancing around. He was digging in his pocket for something.

Brian took a step toward him.

"What's wrong, Gary?"

"The letter." Gary pulled it from his pocket. "I almost forgot about it. Sure hope it ain't wet. Hope I didn't ruin it."

He flipped the brown envelope about, shaking some of the wet off it. Then he dug inside. Brian heard him sigh.

"It's all right. The outside is a little wet, but the letter and the overlay are all right."

"What letter are you talking about?" Odie moved toward them.

Quickly, Gary tucked the letter behind his back. He looked at Brian. Brian shrugged. Odie came closer.

"What you got there, Gary? What did you say about an overlay?"

Brian stepped between Odie and Gary. Gary kept the letter hidden behind his back. Odie was so curious about what Gary had, he almost forgot about the boys being all stinky and wet from falling in the sewer. When he got real close to Brian and took a deep breath, he remembered. That stopped him.

Brian turned to Gary. "I think we ought to tell him," he said, still thinking about Mrs. Becker and how badly he didn't want to go back there.

Gary frowned.

"I . . . I don't know . . . you really think so?"

Brian looked him in the eye and nodded. "I really think so, Gary."

At last, Gary agreed.

When they finally decided to trust somebody, they didn't waste much time telling about the letter Grampa had left and the overlay for the maps. Probably the reason they made the story so short was that they were both cold and wet, and downright sick of the smell.

Odie Ralston was real interested. He kept asking to see the letter and the overlay. But Gary wouldn't let him. He told him about everything that was in the letter and about somebody stealing Grampa's maps and about hearing somebody outside his window the night before. But he wouldn't let Odie get his hands on the letter.

Odie seemed a little disappointed that Gary wouldn't let him have it—"for safekeeping," he'd said. But Gary wasn't about to part with Grampa's letter.

It was then that Brian heard his mom calling from the cabin. He called back, letting her know where he was.

Odie got to fidgeting around—acting nervous or excited or something. Finally, he thanked Gary for telling him about Grampa's letter. He said he still thought Grandpa's drowning was an accident, but after hearing their story, he'd look into it again. Then he jumped into his car and drove off.

Brian stood beside Gary and watched the taillights move off across the bridge. "I got a real bad feeling," he confessed.

Gary frowned. "What about?"

Brian motioned to the cabin. "Your folks and my folks are up there, probably playing cards and visiting—having a right good time. Only, when we come in all wet and smelly, I'm afraid they're

gonna forget what a good time they been havin'
. . . and downright kill us."

Gary's eyes rolled back in his head. He raked
his fingers through his hair again, trying to get
some more of the smelly gunk off. Finally, he
nodded. "I'm afraid you're right. We're really
gonna catch it for this."

Sure enough, they caught it.

Brian never figured his dad and mom could get
so mad at him for anything. But when he and
Gary came walking in, their folks really hit the
ceiling.

Mama rushed around, opening windows and
trying to get the stink out. Gary's mom grabbed
up some newspapers and put them down so the
boys wouldn't drip on the carpet. And their dads
started fussing and yelling at them, using words
that Brian had never heard them use before.

When things finally settled down a bit, their
dads got some soap and marched them down to
Medicine Creek. They made them take off every
stitch of clothing and jump in the river. Gary
knew what they were up to, so he hid the envelope under a rock where he could get it later.
While Brian and Gary were washing up in the ice-
cold water, their dads buried their clothes.

And, as if that wasn't bad enough, when they
got back to the cabin, their mothers told them
they were both grounded for three days. They
couldn't play together or anything!

To Brian, it seemed like an awful hard punishment for accidentally falling in a sewer. It looked like their whole Easter vacation was ruined. If they stayed grounded for three days, vacation would be almost over, and they hadn't gotten to go exploring or fishing or playing cowboys and Indians.

All in all, things were looking pretty bad.

CHAPTER 6

Things started looking a little better Saturday morning, though.

Brian was sitting by the fireplace, next to a little window that looked out across the hillside toward Gary's house. He could see the window in Gary's bedroom. Every now and then, Gary would stick his head out and let Brian know he was still there.

As Brian looked beyond Gary's house to the valley, he could see where the road turned and the path meandered its way up the side of Rattlesnake Hill. He closed his eyes.

With his eyes closed, he could almost see the old witch. The way she came running out of that barn, screaming at them and waving her ax around in the air.

Suddenly, there was a hand on Brian's shoulder. He was thinking—dreaming—about Mrs. Becker. And when the hand touched him, Brian almost jumped straight through the roof.

He managed to catch himself, though. He turned around and saw his dad standing behind him. "Didn't mean to startle you." Dad smiled. "Just wanted to let you know your mom and I are going into Lawton tonight to see a movie. If Gary's folks go with us, you want to spend the night with Gary?"

Brian fought the smile that tugged at the corners of his mouth. "You mean we're not grounded anymore?" he asked.

Dad stroked his chin thoughtfully. "Well, you're still grounded. You're not to leave Gary's house or yard . . . but . . . let's just say you're grounded together."

Brian noticed a little twinkle in his dad's eye when he said that last part.

There wasn't much time. It was only about an hour before dark. Brian and Gary could hardly stand still.

It seemed like it had taken forever for their moms to get ready. And when they finally got their makeup on and their hair all gussied up, it took them even longer to get dressed and start for the car.

Before their parents left, Gary's mom paused on the step and turned toward them. "You two stay close to the house. Remember to feed the dogs. And I expect to find you asleep when we get home—won't be back till late."

Brian's mom was standing beside her. "And stay away from the sewer, too," she added.

Brian felt his eyes roll.

Dad was waiting in the car. He'd been waiting a long time, and he finally was starting to get tired of it. He honked the horn, trying to hurry everyone up.

"We're coming," called Gary's and Brian's moms. Then, they both turned and blew their sons a kiss.

The boys stood real still on the front porch. They waved good-bye. Then they waited until the car pulled out of the driveway, and they kept right on waiting until it was across the bridge. When their folks finally pulled out of sight around the winding road, both of them took off like a shot.

It took about ten seconds to grab their fishing gear and a shovel and head off toward the creek. They had only been grounded for one day, but it seemed like forever. And after being apart, they could hardly wait to get together and go fishing.

Only the fishing wasn't as much fun as they'd hoped. The little perch that filled Medicine Creek just weren't hungry. They wouldn't even try to steal the bait, like they usually did.

About the time the sun sank down behind Mount Scott, Brian and Gary were both fed up with just sitting and not catching anything. They got their fishing gear together and started back toward home.

"Reckon Odie's figured out anything on the car that was around when Grampa got drowned?" Gary asked.

Brian shrugged. "He said that letter was a real good clue. But I figure if he'd found out anything, he woulda told us."

Gary nodded. "It's almost dark. What say we go by his store before we go home."

Brian put his fishing rod over his shoulder. "Okay. Won't hurt to ask him. I've got some change in my jeans. You want to get a Coke and a candy bar while we're there?"

Gary licked his lips. "Sounds great!"

Odie Ralston met them at the front door when they got to his place. He rocked back on his heels and let out that loud, ugly laugh of his.

"Howdy, boys. Say, wasn't that your folks that drove past here about thirty minutes ago?"

Brian nodded. "Yes sir. They're going to a movie in Lawton. We came over to get something to eat."

Brian dug some quarters out of his pocket and handed them to Odie. "This be enough to get a couple of Cokes and a candy bar?"

Odie looked at the money and smiled. "Tell you what, boys. The treat's on me today. You go get what you want. Don't worry about paying. It's my treat."

Brian gave a puzzled look. Finally, he put the

money back in his pocket. When they got over by
the pop machine, Gary nudged him with an elbow.

"Wonder what's wrong with Odie today," he
whispered. "He's so tight with his money, I
didn't figure he'd give his own mother a free
pop."

Brian shrugged. "It sure ain't like him," he
admitted. "But I ain't gonna fuss about it. If he
wants to give us a free pop, that's fine with me."

Suddenly, there was a loud, booming sound—a
crashing, cracking sound followed by a low rumbling. Pops in hand, Brian and Gary rushed over
to the window where Odie was standing. In the
west, they could see a big, black thundercloud
rolling in over the hills. The lightning flashed.
And in a few seconds, the sound of thunder came
roaring and rumbling.

Odie tugged at his shirt collar. "Looks like a
spring storm building up," he said. "Bet it's a
good one, too. Look at all that rain coming
down."

In the distance, Brian could see the dark
streaks of blue where the rain was falling from the
black clouds. It sure was pretty, the way the
sunlight glistened through it, making the dark
lines change shape and color.

Odie rocked back on his heels and stuck his
stomach out. "Yes sir." He laughed. "That one
looks like a real gut-buster. Bet we get might-near
flooded with this one."

The thunder roared again, shaking the plate-glass window in the front of Odie's store.

Gary took a long drink of his pop. "Hurry up and finish," he told Brian. "We better get back to the house before it starts raining here."

Odie scratched at his roly double chin. "Don't worry about finishing your pop," he chuckled. "Go ahead and take the cans with you. You can bring 'em back tomorrow."

Brian shot a puzzled frown at Gary. Gary's eyes popped out real big when he looked at Odie. As tight and stingy as Odie Ralston was, Brian never expected to hear him say something like that. And judging by the way Gary's mouth flopped open, neither did he.

But when the thunder cracked again and the booming roar rattled the plate-glass window in front of Odie's store, Brian didn't hesitate. He headed for the door.

"We'll bring your cans back first thing in the morning, Mr. Ralston," he called. "Come on, Gary, we better git."

They paused on the bridge to talk. But their conversation about Odie's strange, generous behavior wasn't long-lived. The rumbling of the spring thunderstorm urged them on. They ran across the bridge. The old boards clunked and squeaked under their feet.

The wind was whipping and gusting when they reached Gary's house. Buds had already come out on the trees with the warm spring days they'd had. The buds gave the wind something to catch and spin through the air. The branches of trees rattled and whooshed, telling everyone of the coming storm.

Brian left Gary standing at the front door.

"I'll run over to our cabin and get my pajamas. Be right back."

Gary had to fight to hold the screen door against the push of the wind. "All right. I'll see if I can find out anything about the storm on the radio."

"Okay."

Brian ducked his head against the wind and raced off for the cabin.

The cabin was almost dark inside. Brian didn't like going in by himself. Mama and Dad were usually there. This evening, with them in Lawton at the show, the cabin just didn't seem right. It was too quiet and lonely. It was almost spooky without anybody around making noise.

Brian didn't waste any time getting his pajamas. He grabbed his toothbrush from the bathroom and a change of clothes for the morning. At the front door he paused, wondering whether he should lock it or not.

"Wonder if Mama and Dad took their key," he thought.

Suddenly, he heard his name. With a frown, he tilted his head to the side and held his breath, listening.

"Brian . . . Brian!"

The sound was far off and muffled. But he could hear his name. It came again and again above the roar of the coming storm. He turned and looked out the door. It took his eyes a second to adjust to the dim light. He squinted.

There was movement by the front door of Gary's house. Brian opened the screen so he could see better.

The forms took shape.

A huge hulk of a man was dragging Gary. Gary was kicking and struggling, only he wasn't hitting anything but empty air. The huge man dragged him off the front porch and down the stairs. Brian froze, his mouth wide open like his eyes.

Gary kept kicking and yelling. "Brian! Help me. Brian . . . "

The man dragged his friend down the steps like he was as light as a sack of grain. He slung the door of a car open and stuffed Gary inside.

Brian snapped to his senses. He dropped his pajamas and toothbrush. Left them lying in the doorway. Rushed to help.

He couldn't tell who it was, but somebody was kidnapping Gary. Somebody was dragging his best friend from his house and taking him . . . heaven knew where.

Brian charged across the distance between their houses. The sound of a car engine came to his ears.

Brian ran harder. He leaped over rocks that he usually walked around, running as hard as he could. Faster and faster.

But he was too late. There was a roaring sound. Brian got to the driveway just in time to get hit with a faceful of gravel from the spinning tires of a car. It belched up a cloud of dust and gravel behind it and sped onto the road.

The flying rocks stung Brian's face. He had to close his eyes. Cough. He tried to clear away the dust by waving his trembling hands.

Frantic, he raced after the car. But by the time he got out of the dust to where he could see, it was gone. He could hear the engine winding, far down the road. It was out of sight, and he hadn't even had time to get the license number.

Brian blinked, coughing up some more dust. It was like a bad dream. A nightmare. Something was happening that he just couldn't believe.

Why would anyone want to drag Gary off? Why would anyone want to kidnap him?

Brian kept trying to tell himself that any minute he'd wake up. He'd be home in his own bed and Mama would be petting his head and telling him: "It's just a bad dream. Wake up, now."

But he knew it wasn't. It was real. Gary was gone. Someone had kidnapped him. And he, Brian, was left there . . . left there all alone.

CHAPTER 7

Gary's house was cold and lonely without anyone around. Brian stopped when he opened the front door. He stood, squinting into the darkness, holding his breath, listening.

Was anyone else there?

His imagination ran wild. He could picture someone lurking in the shadows, someone waiting to grab him. He imagined a big, ugly man, almost like a monster, with warts all over his face. Sharp teeth like a vampire's. Somebody could be hiding any place in this big house, waiting to grab him and drag him off like they had Gary.

Brian shuddered. The chills raced up his back. Finally, he took a deep breath.

"Quit acting like a scared little kid," he told

himself. "There ain't nobody here. Quit standing around shaking. Go on in. You got to try the phone. You got to get help for Gary."

At last, his trembling fingers found the light. A bright glow flooded the room when he flipped the switch.

The telephone was in the hall. He could see it from where he was. Carefully, looking all around to make sure no one was there, he started toward it. Now he could call for help. He could call into Lawton and tell the police what had happened.

His hands shook as he lifted the receiver. He dialed the operator. There was a long silence. Then a woman's voice: "Hello, this is the Medicine Park operator. May I—"

A loud roar of thunder boomed. Something snapped inside the phone, a loud crack that made Brian drop the phone and grab for his ear.

It took Brian a second to get his senses back. He shook his head. Rubbed at his sore ear. Picked the telephone up again. Dialed.

Nothing happened.

He tapped at the little knobs with his finger. The phone was dead. There was nothing. No humming sound. No buzz. Nothing but the silence. Lightning had struck the line—some place, some place close.

Brian slumped on the stool by the phone, his breath heaving from his tight chest.

He buried his head in his hands. Then he suddenly thought of Odie Ralston.

"Odie," he said. "He'll help me."

In a second, he charged out the front door into a rain that was so thick and heavy it all but blinded him.

But within five minutes, he was back, standing just inside the front door with water dripping from him onto the carpet. Odie was gone. His store was locked up tight and there was no one around the little house in back where he lived.

In a daze, Brian walked through the house. He turned on every light, one after the other, until the whole house was as bright as daytime. Finally, he slumped down on the couch in the living room.

"I'll go crazy if I have to wait here until our folks come home," he thought. "I can't stand waiting. I got to do something. They're gonna go to the movie, then eat out." He shook his head. "Liable to be midnight 'fore they get back."

Suddenly, something caught his eye. On the floor by the couch was an envelope. With a shaking hand, Brian reached out and picked it up. His mouth gaped open. It was the one Gary had shown him four days ago. The one with Grampa's letter and the rice paper overlay inside showing where the Snake Dancer's Gold was.

Brian dug inside. "Empty!" he gasped.

All at once, thoughts started racing through his head. Ideas and memories and all sorts of things that spun round and round, not making any sense at first. Then the mingled, crazy thoughts started piecing together. They started coming clearer and clearer until he finally knew what had happened.

With trembling legs, he walked across the room. He stood looking out the window at the driving rain and listening to the clapping roar of the thunder.

It was all clear now. Whoever had stolen Grampa's maps had found out about the letter he'd left Gary. Someone had waited until their folks left, then they had broken into Gary's house to steal the overlay that showed where the Snake Dancer's Gold was. Gary must have startled them when he came in. And when they took the rice paper overlay, they took Gary, too.

Brian knew what had happened. He knew why that man had kidnapped Gary. And he knew there was only one way he could save his friend.

The fresh smell of spring rain filled his nose as he opened the door. A drumming roar echoed in his ears.

Brian knew what he had to do. It was the last thing in the world he wanted, but he didn't have any choice.

CHAPTER 8

The rain stopped about the time Brian reached the swinging bridge. The boards made a clunking sound as he moved across them. In the center of the bridge, he paused and stared down at the moonlight shimmering on the ripples in the creek.

There was a sound of thunder rumbling in the distance. The big steel cable that held the swinging bridge swayed with the gentle breeze that followed the raging storm.

Brian squeezed the cable. Squeezed hard. Squeezed until his knuckles turned white.

The thunder roared again. It was closer this time than before. Brian glanced up. In the evening sky, he could see the huge banks of black clouds that rolled about the peak of Mount Scott.

There was another storm coming, another big

one. It was rolling over the mountains, only a few minutes behind the last one.

A lump came to Brian's throat. For a moment, he couldn't move. Then he was off again, walking with a slow, determined stride, on legs that were so tired they didn't even shake and tremble anymore.

After a while, Brian came to the narrow path leading up the side of Rattlesnake Hill. It wound and twisted its way into a dark forest where the trees and vines grabbed at his clothes. The leaves were so thick he couldn't see the stars overhead.

Brian moved on, slowly. In his mind's eye, he could picture the huge brown house that stood at the end of the path. The house and the rickety barn. The old witch with the tangled, white hair that spun and twisted like the web of an angry spider.

Mrs. Becker was his only hope. She was the only one who knew where the Snake Dancer's Cave was. Whoever had kidnapped Gary had taken him there.

Brian swallowed hard. Much as he hated to, much as the fear raged up inside him, he had to go back to where that crazy old witch had chased him with her ax.

The thunder roared loudly. It was close enough to shake the heavy, damp air all around him. The wind blew harder as the storm closed in.

Brian felt like his feet were made of lead. But

he forced himself to go on. Forced himself to fight back against the fear that raged up inside him.

When he stepped into the clearing around Mrs. Becker's house, the storm inside him was almost raging out of control.

Lightning flashed above.

He could feel his heart pounding in his ears and his breath coming in short gasps.

The lightning lit up the sky and the ground. The big house loomed in front of him. Lonely and still, it seemed to wait for him to come. Quietly, like some great, sleeping monster, it stood, daring him to draw nearer.

Thunder followed the flash of light. It was strong. It seemed to slam the wind against his chest, almost knocking the air from his tight lungs.

As Brian stepped to the porch, the thunder died away. For a second, the wind seemed to stop. The rustling of the trees stood still, swallowed by an ominous silence.

Brian's hand trembled as he raised his fist to knock. The sound of his knocking was almost loud enough to wake the dead. He waited, but only a second—only long enough for the silence to close in before he knocked again.

The door flew open. Bright lights from inside almost blinded him. He blinked.

"What are you doing here?" a tight, angry voice demanded.

Brian opened his mouth, only nothing came out. The light from behind Mrs. Becker made her tangled, white hair shine and sparkle with a ghostly glow. A glistening of light caught Brian's eye. In her right hand, he saw a butcher knife.

"I warned you kids not to come back." She shook the knife at him. "I chased you off once. Now . . ."

She stopped talking for a second. Her angry face softened to a confused frown. "My Lord, child. You're soaked clean to the bone. Why on earth would you be prowling around here on a night like this? You'll catch your death."

Brian swallowed. He'd forgotten about being cold and wet. All he could think of was that gleaming butcher knife in Mrs. Becker's hand.

"Mrs. Becker, I'm Brian, Gary's friend. Help me. Please."

She took a step toward him. For a moment, it seemed like she was trying to look past him. She frowned. Shook the knife in his face.

"This ain't no trick, is it? You boys ain't trying to pull something?"

"No."

"What are you doing here?"

"Mrs. Becker . . . please . . . help me."

Brian blinked. He stopped talking and started to cry. He didn't want to. He hated himself for doing it. Only he was so scared and so confused and so lonely that there wasn't any way he could keep from it. He felt the warmth of the tears as they rolled down his cheek. The bitterness as the salty water reached the side of his mouth. He didn't care what happened to him anymore.

Suddenly, there was a soft, comforting hand on his shoulder—a warm, gentle, understanding hand that drew him close.

"There, there, honey." Mrs. Becker's voice was soft and kind. "You hush your cryin', now. Tell me what's wrong. I'll help. It'll be all right. Don't you cry, now."

Mrs. Becker was a lot different than Brian had thought. When he finally told her what had happened and why he was here, she went right off to get her raincoat and a couple of flashlights.

As they walked down the path from Rattlesnake Hill, she told him some things about herself that helped him understand why she acted the way she did.

Like Grampa had said in his letter, Mrs. Becker's husband had died eight years before when he was hunting for the Snake Dancer's Gold. And she figured somebody had killed him, just like what happened to Grampa. Somebody broke into her house, too, looking for maps. But when they didn't find them, they broke in again and again. That was when Mrs. Becker started staying home instead of going out with friends, like most folks did. And when she started staying home, some of the kids in town got the idea she was a witch and started pestering her.

Brian couldn't understand how a woman as old

77

as Mrs. Becker was as spry as she was. When she got the flashlights and took off toward town, Brian almost had to run to keep up with her. By the time they reached the old hotel, he was puffing for breath and almost tuckered out.

"Can we slow down some?" he puffed.

Mrs. Becker nodded. "We'll slow up a bit," she said. "But from what you've told me, your friend's in a heap of trouble. If we don't hurry, you might not have a friend at all."

The second thunderstorm was right on their heels. The wind whipped and tossed Mrs. Becker's stringy white hair. When they walked under one of the streetlights, her hair seemed to turn almost blue. Mrs. Becker glanced up at the light.

"You best turn your flashlight out," she said. "The batteries are pretty old. It might not last."

Brian clicked the light off with his thumb. He glanced back over his shoulder when he heard a clap of thunder.

"You reckon we can find the Snake Dancer's Cave before that storm hits?"

Mrs. Becker smiled. "I don't think we can even make it, without some transportation. Come on."

Brian followed her toward the center of the little town.

"Near as I can remember," she said, "the cave is about seven miles from here. We got to go out the highway about a mile past the Y. Then off into the hills for quite a ways."

Brian glanced over his shoulder.

"Maybe we could flag down a car. Have somebody give us a ride."

Mrs. Becker laughed. "The way we look, I doubt that anybody'd pick us up. 'Sides, there ain't much traffic tonight."

Brian's shoulders sagged. "Then what *are* we gonna do?"

Mrs. Becker waved the flashlight, telling him to follow.

"We'll see," she answered. "I got me an idea— but we'll have to see."

It was a long time before they reached the café and beer joint on the highway, just outside of town. The sound of the jukebox blared from inside. Brian could hear people talking and laughing. The sound of pool balls clattering together came from the billiard table near the window.

When they got to the café, Mrs. Becker stopped. It took a second for her to catch her breath. She walked slowly, weaving in and out between the cars that were parked in front of the place.

When she passed the last car, she heaved a sigh. "Just what I was afraid of. Them drunk people inside must have been sober when they got here. They all took their keys out of the cars."

Brian felt his eyes pop. "You mean you was gonna steal a car?"

79

Mrs. Becker shrugged.

"No, just borrow it. I was even gonna honk the horn. Let folks know I was taking it and try to get a crowd following us. But all them dang fools had to go and take their keys."

Suddenly, her face broke into a wide grin. She pointed a crooked finger toward the side of the café. "Well, lookie there. I think we're in luck."

Brian looked where she was pointing. There, leaned up against the side of the building, was a motorcycle. Grinning like a kid who'd just found a toy under a Christmas tree, Mrs. Becker trotted over to it.

"Ain't seen one of these contraptions in years." She knelt down for a closer look at the motor. Scratched her head. She thought aloud: "I wonder if I still remember how . . . "

Brian took a step back. He frowned. "You ain't thinkin' about swiping that motorcycle?"

Mrs. Becker ignored him. She waved a hand for him to come closer. "Hold that flashlight of yours down here. It's been so long, I don't know if I remember how to do this."

Brian clicked on the light for her. "Do what?" he asked.

Mrs. Becker tugged on one of the wires by the starter.

"Hot-wire the thing. The key's gone. But if I can recall how to cross over these ignition wires, we can still get 'er going."

"We ain't gonna steal a motorcycle—are we?"

"Hold the light still, boy."

"I mean . . . " Brian stuttered. "You could kill both of us on that thing. We could . . . I mean . . . er . . . you don't know how to drive . . . er, ride one of them, do you?"

Mrs. Becker kept fiddling with the wires.

"Listen, sonny," Mrs. Becker said over her shoulder. "These contraptions aren't as modern as you think. I was riding one of these cycles long 'fore you was born." She kept talking as she worked with the wires. "Chancy and I got our oldest son an Indian 750 cycle when he graduated from high school. Week after he got it, he lost the key. Anytime we wanted to go any place, we had to hot-wire the darn thing."

Her old knees popped when she straightened up. "There," she brushed her hands together. "That ought to do it."

Brian couldn't believe his eyes. Mrs. Becker hiked her dress up and swung it over the seat. She turned the controls back and forth and found the clutch with her foot. Then, she smiled and patted the seat behind her. "Hop on. Let's give 'er a try."

Brian shook his head. "I . . . er . . . I don't know."

Mrs. Becker shrugged. "Well, to be real truthful"—she smiled—"I don't know either. It's been a long time. They've changed the transmission

81

and probably the differential from the old models I used to ride. But I think I can work the fool thing."

Brian swallowed hard. "Are you sure?"

"Well, Brian, my husband, Chancy, said ridin' a cycle was just like swimmin'. Once you learn, you never forget. If I forgot, it won't take us long to find out. Worse we can do is end up in the creek if I'm wrong."

Brian's forehead wrinkled into a frown. He didn't think of Mrs. Becker as being a witch anymore. He just couldn't figure a woman of her age jumping on a motorcycle, much less a stolen one. But there she was, sitting and patting the seat behind her for him to get on.

Brian heaved a long, worried sigh. Then he was on behind her.

"Hang on round my waist," she said.

Brian got hold of her. She jumped down on the pedal with her foot. The cycle sputtered, then died. Again, she tried it.

Brian glanced at the night sky. *Dear Lord,* he said to himself. *I ain't asked for much—but I sure hope you don't let her kill us on this motorcycle.*

Mrs. Becker jumped on the pedal about five more times, in quick order. The door of the café flew open. A young man with a helmet under his arm came running out.

"Hey!" he screamed. "What are you doing on my cycle? Hey—"

Mrs. Becker jumped another time. The roaring

putter of the engine drowned out the man's angry voice. Brian glanced over his shoulder. The man came racing toward them, shaking his fist in the air. His mouth was moving ninety-to-nothing, and Brian was glad the motor was drowning out the words he must be saying.

All of a sudden, the cycle leaped forward. Brian felt his neck pop back. He grabbed tight to Mrs. Becker's skirt. The cycle leaped again, weaving from side to side. Brian just knew she was going to kill them both.

The cycle bounced up and down. It surged forward, then slowed to almost stopping, as Mrs. Becker tried to figure out how to make the throttle work.

She fought the handlebars. The cycle whipped from side to side. Brian closed his eyes. Mrs. Becker kept sticking one leg out, then the other, to keep the cycle from turning over. Each time, it jerked like it was fixing to flip clean over on top of them.

But lo and behold, after all the jerking and jolting and jostling, they went racing up the hill and off into the night.

The wind spun Brian's hair. It whistled in his ears and felt cool against his cheeks. They topped the hill and turned onto the highway. There was a car coming from the opposite direction as Mrs. Becker whipped the cycle onto the road. The car squealed its brakes and honked, just barely missing them. Brian had to close his eyes again. Then he could hear Mrs. Becker yelling at him. The wind was racing by so fast, he could barely hear her. He leaned forward.

"What?" he screamed into the roaring wind.

Mrs. Becker leaned back so he could hear. "Can't figure out where the danged lights are. Hold your flashlight over my shoulder so we can see where we're going."

Brian's hands were shaking so hard, he didn't think he was ever going to get the light out of his jeans.

It was about then that Brian changed his mind again about Mrs. Becker. Folks were right. She *was* crazy.

She'd have to be crazy. Here they were sailing down the highway in the dark, doing a good seventy miles an hour, on a stolen motorcycle, and with no headlight, yet.

Then Brian figured that he must be crazy, too. Here he was with her. Holding the flashlight over her shoulder so they could see the pavement whizzing past. He had to allow for it, though, seeing as how his best friend's life might be in danger. Maybe it was all right to be a little crazy when the situation was as desperate as this one.

CHAPTER 9

About a mile past the Wichita Mountain Y, Mrs. Becker slowed the cycle. She drove with one hand. With her other she took the flashlight. She waved it back and forth on the side of the road.

"It's been twelve years since I been around here, but I bet I'll remember the trail mark if I see it."

She kept shining the light. The cycle kept moving slower and slower, until finally it stopped. Mrs. Becker let it idle, shining her light on a big cottonwood tree close to the road. There was a long diamond-shaped boulder leaning up against the side of the tree. Finally, she glanced over her shoulder. "This is it, Brian. That marks the creek bed that leads to the Snake Dancer's Cave. Hang on."

The cycle jumped forward again. Brian clung tight to her waist. They roared right past the cottonwood tree—only inches from it. They bounced some when they left the road. And, on the other side of the tree, Mrs. Becker turned sharply and almost flipped them. But instead of turning over, they ended up in a dry creek bed and went racing on.

Brian leaned close to Mrs. Becker's ear.

"You think we ought to slow down?" he pleaded.

Mrs. Becker shook her head. "Creek's flat for about a quarter of a mile. I'll slow down when we leave the creek and start climbing toward the cliff."

So they raced on. Raced over the small rocks in the bottom of the creek. Swished past the huge boulders of solid granite rock that poked from the banks on either side. Roared under the low-hanging limbs of trees that kept them ducking and weaving from side to side. And Mrs. Becker didn't slow down one little bit.

Things went just fine—for a while.

Then there was a loud, twanging sound. Brian felt the cycle stop dead, only he and Mrs. Becker kept right on going.

All of a sudden, he was flying in the air. Something hit his foot. He lost his grip on Mrs. Becker and went flying off in a direction all by himself, while Mrs. Becker went flying in another.

Things flipped over and over—upside-down and crossways. Then he went sliding into the ground. The little rocks along the side of the creek bit at his shoulder and leg. He was thankful that it had rained earlier. The water had made the creek bed muddy. It made his fall softer.

After a minute, when things stopped spinning, Brian sat up and looked around. The motorcycle engine had died after the crash. Everything was quiet. Brian just knew Mrs. Becker was dead. She was too old to take a fall like that.

Then, all of a sudden, he heard an angry muttering.

"Ruined," the voice growled. "Danged sloppy mud. Best dress I own, and now it's ruined."

Brian looked around. Mrs. Becker was standing a few feet away. She shined her light down on her dress and was trying to scrape some of the mud off.

She was muddy from head to toe. Her dress was torn in a couple of places, but other than that, she looked as spry as ever. After working to get the mud off for a time, she finally gave up. She turned her light back to where the cycle had wrecked.

"Darned fool farmer. Who'da thought some crazy farmer would string a new fence across that creek?" She turned the light on Brian. "You all right, boy?"

"Yes ma'am."

"Good. You was right." She came over and helped him to his feet. "I should have slowed down like you said. We musta been doing at least forty when we hit that barbed-wire fence. I sure didn't know any farmer had put that fence up. Sorry."

Brian brushed himself off.

"That's all right. Are you sure you're not hurt?"

"Nope. I'm fine. Couple of bruises. That's all." She turned the light around, trying to get her bearings. She scratched her head and shrugged. "Ain't sure, but I think it's this way. Come on. We're only about a half-mile away now."

Brian followed her out of the creek bed and onto the rock-covered ground beyond the banks. It seemed like most of the time they were climbing. They'd top a small hill, then walk down into a little valley, then struggle up a higher hill.

Mrs. Becker set a good pace. Her old legs carried her smoothly over the rocky ground. Brian had to work to keep up with her. But after a while the climbing began to slow her down. In front of him, Brian could hear her breathing. Her air came in shorter and shorter gasps. Finally, she had to stop and rest.

"Just not as young as I used to be," she puffed. Brian tried to make her stay there and rest, but before he knew it, she was on her feet again.

In the distance, Brian could hear the storm.

The rumbling of the thunder seemed to roll and echo from the hills around them, a constant roaring, like the thunder was going to last forever.

They came to a steep part in the hill. Brian shined his light and found a straight cliff. It looked impossible to climb. But instead of going up it, Mrs. Becker turned sharply to the right. In a minute, they were back in the creek bed. They followed it to the base of the cliffs. There, the creek had cut a narrow gorge in the rocks. It was deep and slanted, yet there were plenty of handholds and footholds, so they could climb.

As they climbed, Brian shined his light all around. In some places, giant boulders had fallen from the tops of the cliff and wedged about halfway down in the deep gorge, blotting out the night sky. In other places, there were so many of them clumped above, they blocked out the flashes of light from the coming storm.

Finally, they reached the top of the gorge. Mrs. Becker was puffing and panting like she was fixing to drop. It took her a long time to catch her breath.

"We best be quiet from here on," she whispered. "Whoever stole Gary's grandpa's map is probably already at the cave. I just pray your friend is still with them, and that he's still all right."

A big boulder blocked the end of the gorge. They had to climb around it, struggling and straining to reach the top. Brian got to the top of the big rock first. He leaned down and helped Mrs. Becker up. Then he turned to see where they were.

The lightning flashed in a long, twisting finger that raced across the whole sky. The light lasted long enough for Brian to see what was in front of them.

A green, flat valley opened just beyond the gorge. It was about as big as a football field, only round instead of squared off. On all sides, sheer rock cliffs rose toward the black sky. They were as smooth and straight as if some giant had taken a knife and sliced them off. At the far end of the meadow, there was a big tree beside a pool of water.

"There," Mrs. Becker whispered. "Where the cliffs rise up behind that big tree. Come on." She tugged at his elbow, leading him along a little stream that twisted its way from the pool to the edge of the gorge where they stood.

Brian didn't realize how strange and eerie the place was until they started walking across the meadow. The lightning flashed and rumbled again. Brian could see then just how high the cliffs were. They completely surrounded the small valley. Tall and sharp, they seemed to cut the valley off from everywhere else on the face of the earth. It was a place all alone, different from any other in the whole world.

The sheer cliffs caught the roaring boom of the thunder. The sound bounced from the towering walls. Clattered and rumbled. Made the ground shake beneath their feet.

A sudden flash of lightning came close, just above the cliffs. Brian froze, startled and frightened by the bright light and the following roar that hurt his ears.

Mrs. Becker reached out her hand and took his. She stood there and waited.

Another flash of lightning came. She pointed to the tree. Just above it, Brian could see the gaping hole in the face of the rock cliff. The lightning lit up everything else. Only the mouth of the cave stayed dark, black as death itself.

Mrs. Becker leaned close. "This is the sacred Valley of the Snake Dancer," she whispered.

The lightning came again. She pointed up to the cave. "And that—the Indians used to call it Death Cave."

Brian felt the chills race up his back. His hair bristled out on his neck. He could barely breathe. He had the feeling that eyes were watching him. He could see no one else around, yet still he had that feeling. That burning, cold feeling of eyes on the back of his neck. Eyes that were there, but not there. Sounds behind him. Sounds that stopped when he turned to look. And there was a cold, icy feeling down deep in the pit of his stomach.

This was the sacred place of the Snake Dancers. Probably, in all of time, no more than a handful of white men had ever set eyes on the place. And as Grampa's story raced over and over in Brian's mind, he realized that none of the white people that had seen the place lived to tell about it.

CHAPTER 10

It was like walking through a dream as Mrs. Becker and Brian made their way across the valley to the oak tree at the base of the cliff. The rain from the storm had started. A light, misty kind of rain. A drizzle that dampened the air and made everything look fuzzy. Like the haze of a dream. Like the blurry, frightening fog of a nightmare.

Brian blinked. The haze remained. He blinked again, rubbing his eyes.

"Stop a minute," Mrs. Becker's voice whispered from behind him. "Got to rest."

Brian glanced back. Mrs. Becker leaned against a large granite slab. She held herself there, puffing for air. Even in the faint glow of the fading moonlight, he could see the flush of her cheeks. She sat fanning her face with one hand.

Brian frowned, worried. "Are you gonna be all right?"

Mrs. Becker was quick to nod. "In a minute. Just not used to all this . . . climbing. Been a long time."

Brian sat down near her to wait. The rain had started now. He pulled at his collar, trying to keep the cold drops from rolling off his wet hair and down his back. It was a slow, easy rain, the kind that soaks deep into the ground, the kind that soaks you clean to the bone.

In a few minutes, Mrs. Becker was on her feet. She motioned with a shake of her wet head. "We can get out of this once we reach the cave. Come on."

The climbing was harder, now. It was steep and slippery with the rain. Twice, they took the wrong path. They followed cuts in the rock. Places where the sheer rock cliff had caved in, probably centuries ago, and left fallen boulders and knobs of sharp rock for them to cling to. But both times, the cuts in the rock played out. They came to dead-ends at the face of the cliff, with nothing beyond them but sheer, straight walls.

Again they backed up. They tried another ridge of rock that was more narrow and slippery-looking than the two before.

The mouth of the cave was hidden for a long

time. The huge boulders of granite that jutted out from the face of the cliff stood between them and the hole in the wall. Then it was in front of them. Still, there was a steep climb along a narrow ledge. Brian felt his heart race. They were almost to the opening. It was just a little farther.

"Darned . . . blasted . . . slippery . . . "

He turned to Mrs. Becker when he heard her voice. She was down on her hands and knees on the narrow ledge. Brian rushed back to her.

"What is it? You hurt?"

Mrs. Becker didn't answer. Finally, she turned and sat down on the path, rubbing her knee.

Brian knelt beside her. "What? Did you fall? What is it?"

She straightened her leg out. "Darned slippery rocks," she growled. "Landed right square on that kneecap."

Brian's forehead wrinkled up when he frowned. "Did you break it?"

Mrs. Becker put her hand on her knee, wiggling it back and forth just a little.

"Nope. Sure knocked the tar out of it, though. I'm kind of winded, too. Ain't near as young as I used to be. I'll be okay in a minute."

Brian frowned. "Are you sure? Really sure?"

Mrs. Becker nodded. "Yes. Help me to that rock over there. Looks like the storm's picking up."

Brian held her arm and walked with her to a big

boulder that hung out over the path. The falling rain rolled down the big stone and dripped off the front. But there was a spot near the center where the ground was dry and out of the weather. Mrs. Becker sat there and smiled. "I'll be all right in a few minutes." She glanced up the path, twisting her wrinkled mouth into a worried frown. Then she glanced up at the darkening sky and watched the rain pour down in sheets. She watched the lightning flash, making the streams of rain shine.

"Maybe you better go on to the cave alone," she said finally. "Do you think you can make it by yourself?"

Brian pushed his shoulders back. "Yes. But . . . are you sure you're all right?"

She smiled. "I'll be fine. Listen. You be quiet. If you hear voices or see anything, you come hightailing it back here. You understand? Don't try to do nothin' by yourself. Just go up there and check if anyone's around."

She shook her head and heaved a sigh. "This whole thing might be a wild goose chase," she admitted. "There might not be nobody up there at all. But if there is, we need to know who and how many. You just go find out and come straight back."

Brian nodded quickly. "I will, Mrs. Becker. I won't do anything but go look. I'll be right back."

He eased to his feet and started up the path. The flashlight seemed dimmer than before. But he figured it was all the rain that made it hard to see.

He ducked his head. Moved on slow, careful feet up the smooth rock trail.

The path grew more narrow the farther he went. The last few feet to the cave, he had to stuff the light in his back pocket so he could hang on with both hands. Once, he glanced over his shoulder at what was below. It was only about twenty to thirty feet to the ground. But it was a straight drop, and there was nothing below but sharp, jagged rocks.

A few feet farther, and he was above the top of the large oak tree that stood beside the pool down in the meadow. With all the rain, Brian couldn't tell if the pool of water was deep or not.

Suddenly, the trail in front of him disappeared. Brian held on to the ledge and waited for another bright flash of lightning so he could look around.

When the lightning came again, he found the path. Instead of following the ledge, it made a sharp turn and went almost straight up. It looked like lots of water had flowed down the cut at one time, because the rocks were worn smooth and there were little rumples and rills in the stone. The climbing wasn't hard. Brian pulled himself up, hand over hand. And when he finally pulled himself over a smooth, rounded rock, he found he was staring straight into the gaping black mouth of Death Cave.

It wasn't nearly as big as it looked from the valley below. When Brian stood in it, he had to lean over to keep from hitting his head on the top.

The entrance to the cave was perfectly round. It was like standing in the end of a huge, dark barrel. He grabbed the flashlight from his back pocket and stepped farther into the opening, where he would be out of the wind-driven rain.

Brian held his breath, listening. There was no sound but the pounding of the storm outside. He would have to go deeper into the cave to hear if anyone was there. He turned the flashlight on. Took a breath.

The odor that came to his nose was a heavy, musky smell. He coughed, but quickly closed his mouth so as not to make any sound. He sniffed at the air again, trying to figure out what the strange smell was.

He had to go on. He had to move farther into the cave so he would be away from the sound of the storm.

The entrance way kept its round shape for about ten feet. It was like walking into the smooth, round mouth of a giant cannon. Then, suddenly, the ceiling rose up.

Brian straightened, shining the light around above him. The top of the cave was well over twenty feet high here. The top and sides were all covered with small holes.

He was standing in a smooth trough of solid rock no taller than his shoulders. There was a flat ledge on both sides of the trough, about four feet wide. When he stretched his arms out, he could almost touch the ledges on either side.

Beyond the ledge, the walls of the cave curved up to meet the roof. Everything, except the trough where he stood, was honeycombed with those small round holes.

He paused a moment. Held his breath. Listened.

The sound of the storm rolled in through the entrance of the cave. He shined his light in front of him. Brian knew he had to go deeper into the cave. He knew he had to get farther from the storm if he expected to hear anything besides the roar and rumble of the thunder.

Brian moved forward on catlike feet. He came down softly on the smooth, solid rock. He didn't make a sound.

He followed the trough. It was straight for a ways. Then it began to twist and turn. Once again, it straightened out. About ten yards ahead, at the end of the straight part, the trough turned sharply to the left.

When Brian reached the corner, he shined his flashlight so he could see what was ahead. The light was getting very dim. He had to stare to see what was there.

The cave closed down into a narrow opening, something like the entrance. It was a small, round tunnel that turned to the right. Again, Brian had to stoop down to follow the path through the narrow tunnel. And again, after a few yards, the narrow tunnel opened into a larger cavern. But this one wasn't like the one near the entrance. All the walls were smooth here. It was like being on the inside of a giant ball that was hollowed out.

There were drawings on the walls. Pictures. Dark places where the soot from fires had blackened the rock.

It was as if Brian had crawled through a tunnel and come out in another world. A world of a hundred years ago. A private world that belonged only to the Indians. A strange, eerie world that told of the sacred Snake Dancers. A place where he didn't belong. Where he wasn't welcome.

CHAPTER 11

Brian shook his flashlight, and the light became a little brighter. He could look around for a second and study the pictures and drawings in the room.

The sound of the storm was silenced by the rock walls. The only noise was his own breathing. It made the cave even scarier than before.

The drawings were as big as life—some of them so well drawn that Brian shuddered, like he was looking at a real Indian instead of just an ancient drawing of one. There were pictures of Indians on horses, and of buffalo. There were drawings of Indians dancing around a fire with war paint on and lances in their hands.

On the right side of the cave were pictures of the Snake Dancers. That's what they had to be, Brian decided. The Indians wore buffalo headdresses—the skulls of buffalo with the horns and hair still on them. Brian could only see a little of the dancers' faces—down below where the masks came. They each held snakes in their hands. The way the pictures were drawn, with the men in different positions, Brian could almost see them moving. He could almost picture them dancing around the cave, making their ceremonies and magic about the fires.

The snakes looked like they would start wiggling any minute. Wiggle themselves right off the walls and come slithering and crawling toward him. Brian moved the light on around to the far side of the cave, where the drawing of an enormous Indian reached almost to the roof. Powerful muscles seemed to ripple as Brian moved his light across the drawing. The Indian stood with legs apart. The small opening to another tunnel stood between the Indian's feet. Brian started toward it, then stopped to look up at the gigantic figure.

The Indian stood defiant and proud, like he was guarding the tunnel between his feet, warning anyone who might enter not to go there. Like the others, he wore a buffalo headdress and robe. In his hands, he clutched a giant rattlesnake. A smaller snake was laid across his shoulders, and the Indian held its neck in his mouth. Just above the entrance to the tunnel was another snake. It was so perfectly drawn that Brian could see its fangs—and they were partly buried in the Indian's leg!

Brian felt such a big knot in his throat that he had trouble swallowing.

The picture was almost as frightening as the silence of the cave. He wanted to run. Hurry back outside to Mrs. Becker. Run away to where he wouldn't be alone and could feel safe.

Instead, he went on—straight to the tunnel that the giant Indian guarded. The only feeling stronger than the fear that boiled inside him was curiosity. Something was drawing him on, calling him deeper into the sacred cave.

Again, he had to bend down to squeeze through the tunnel. This one was longer than the others. It sloped upward. Not much, but Brian could feel that he was climbing.

Instead of opening suddenly into a large chamber, the tunnel he was in widened slowly, growing larger and larger as he moved. Brian finally found himself in a huge chamber. Like the ones near the entrance, this one was honeycombed with small, round holes all about the walls. There were small caves that went off to the sides, branching out like the limbs of a tree.

For a moment, Brian felt lost. Confused. He didn't know which way to go, which branch of the cave to follow. Then he looked down. The floor was covered with dust here, instead of solid rock. And in the dust he saw footprints. There was the large, deep track of a man. Beside it, there was the smaller, lighter footprint of a boy.

Brian froze. He held his breath. Listened.

There wasn't a sound.

Quiet as he could, he started following the tracks. They led deeper into the cave, past twisting and curving outcrops of rock. Again, he came to solid rock under his feet. But this part of the cave wasn't branched like the part he had just left. There was only one trail to follow. He moved on.

Then he was as far as he could go. There was a big chamber with nothing but solid rock on the other side from where he had entered. He shined the light around. There were no tunnels. No branches. This was the end of the cave.

Brian frowned, figuring he must have followed the wrong path. Then he remembered where he had last seen the footprints in the sand. He couldn't have taken the wrong path. This had to be the way they had come.

He moved the light around, trying to find some clue to where the tracks might have gone. Something beside him caught his eye.

But when he turned to look, his flashlight went out.

Frantically, he slapped it against his other hand. The light came on again, but it was weak. The little light it gave off made things hard to see.

Suddenly, Brian froze. He stopped stark-still, trembling so hard he almost fell. Along the side of the cave, he saw what had caught his eye.

Bones!

Skeletons!

His eyes grew wide. Chills raced up his spine. Set the hair at the back of his neck tingling with fear. They were skeletons of people. Skulls, with mouths opened in terror and with fingers laid across their chest or face, just as they had frozen in death.

The bodies were twisted. Some were laid across one another, others doubled against the wall of the cave, like the men had crawled there to escape something too horrible to imagine.

Brian couldn't count them, there were so many. He forced himself to be brave. Made himself study that side of the cave. He tried to find a way that the tracks might have gone. Tried to ignore the skeletons—but he couldn't.

He hadn't looked far when his flashlight flickered.

He slapped it against his hand, only this time, it didn't come back on. He hit it again.

It was no use. The batteries were dead. His light was gone! He was alone in the dark. Alone with the skeletons of the dead.

He didn't want to go on now. He didn't care to see strange, new things that no one else had ever seen. All the curiosity was gone from him. All he wanted was to get out.

Only he couldn't. He'd come too far into the cave to ever get out without a light. He was trapped there.

Trapped in the dark, silent tomb of Death Cave!

CHAPTER 12

Brian would have screamed. He would have crumpled on the floor of the cave and crawled away from the skeletons. He would have fought the darkness with his fist, clawed it with his hands.

Only he didn't have time.

Just as Brian's flashlight went out, he heard a sound. It was a soft, far-off sound, a sound he could barely hear at first. But it was a sound that didn't belong in a place where everything was dead and still.

It was the sound of someone crying.

Brian frowned. Tilted his head to the side. Listened to the sound for a long time—just to make sure of what it was. Then he started toward it. Crawled on his hands and knees. Felt his way through the pitch dark. Prayed he wouldn't accidentally crawl over one of those skeletons. He crawled toward the back of the chamber, where he had seen only solid rock before.

The sound of the crying grew louder.

Then, as he came closer, the sound changed. It was like it was coming from all around him. Below. Above. From all sides. Brian tilted his head to the side. He couldn't tell where the voice was anymore.

He did recognize it now, though. A smile came to his face. "Gary," he called into the darkness.

The crying stopped.

"Gary? Is that you?"

"Brian?"

"Yes. Gary, where are you?"

"Brian, is that really you?" Gary's voice cried out for him. "How did you find me? Where are you?"

"I'm coming," Brian answered. "Just keep talking. I'll find you."

"No," Gary warned. "I'm in a pit. Don't come any closer."

His friend's warning was too late. Brian reached out with his hands. There was nothing there but empty space. He tried to catch himself, but there was nothing to grab.

He fell forward. The blackness spun around. He twisted and struggled against the empty air until he hit the bottom. Silver stars spun before his eyes. Then everything went black. He felt as cold as the cave's floor itself as he lost consciousness.

There were voices, faraway voices, like those heard in a dream. A soft, loving hand caressed the place on the back of his head where it hurt so bad. Brian tried to open his eyes, but he couldn't.

The spinning and throbbing in his head eased some. The far-off voices came closer.

"I think he's coming around now," Mrs. Becker's voice said.

"Good." He heard Gary sigh. "I just knew for sure he'd killed himself when he fell."

Brian forced his eyes open. It was light. He saw Mrs. Becker sitting above him. She held his head in her lap and rubbed at the big knot on the back of his skull. Gary sat on his other side. He smiled when he saw Brian look up at him.

"How you feel?"

Brian tried to sit up. The throbbing in his head forced him back down.

"I don't know," he moaned. "What happened?"

"You fell off the edge up there," Gary pointed.

Brian looked up. They were surrounded by solid rock. Smooth and straight, it went up for about fifteen feet. He blinked again.

"Where are we? What happened?"

Mrs. Becker helped him sit up.

"We're down in the bottom of a pit. I figure it's

a skunk hole," she said. "Judging by that stinkin' critter up above us."

Brian looked up. A lantern hung over the top of the pit. Odie Ralston's fat, ugly face glared down at them.

"All right," his gruff voice boomed. "He's all right. You two get back to work."

Brian struggled to get up on his knees.

"What happened?"

Mrs. Becker got to her feet. She dusted her dress off with her hands. "I got to worryin' about you, when you didn't come out," she said. "Came in to see what had happened to you. If I'd a waited a few more minutes, I woulda seen Odie sneaking up the path outside. He came into the cave right after I did. Sneaked up behind me and grabbed me. Then he lowered me down here in this pit."

Brian shook his head. He tried to get to his feet, but the bump he'd gotten on his head left him too weak to stand.

"Why?" he wondered. "Why'd he put us here?"

Mrs. Becker stepped to the side, pointing behind her. There, with them in the bottom of the deep pit, were five huge wooden crates.

"Gold," Mrs. Becker answered as she pointed to the boxes. "The Snake Dancer's Gold."

Brian felt his mouth drop open.

"I mean it," Odie's voice boomed again. "Get back to work."

Mrs. Becker patted Brian on the shoulder. "You rest awhile, son. We won't be far."

Brian leaned against the smooth, slick wall of the pit. Mrs. Becker and Gary walked over to the big wooden crates and started pulling out sacks. The sacks tinkled and jingled with the movement of the gold coins inside them. Odie lowered a long rope from the edge. Then he dropped down about eight strands of nylon cord. Mrs. Becker and Gary went to work tying the sacks onto the big rope with the cord. When they'd used all of it, Odie pulled it up, making grunting sounds. There was some more rattling around as he moved the gold. Then the light from his lantern grew dim. Once again it was dark in the cave.

Brian felt fear grip him when the darkness came. He called out for Gary and Mrs. Becker.

"We're right here, boy," Mrs. Becker answered.

Suddenly, there was a light. Mrs. Becker shined her flashlight on herself, then on Gary.

"Odie did leave me my flashlight."

They both came over to sit beside Brian. Mrs. Becker started shining the light around the pit.

"Odie's gone a bunch of times to carry the gold out of the cave. I figure he's got a couple of packhorses tied some place down below. Both times he's gone, me and Gary's tried to figure us a way out of here. Ain't had much luck."

Brian's eyes followed the spot of light around the pit. The walls were smooth as glass and straight up. There wasn't a single knob of rock or a handhold or crack where they could climb out. The top of the pit was more than fifteen feet straight up. Way too far to jump.

Mrs. Becker clicked the light off. Brian could hear her heave a sigh as she settled back against the side of the pit. "Looks pretty hopeless, don't it? Well, maybe we can figure us a way out of here after he's gone."

In the darkness, they sat for a time, all three trying to think of a way to get out of their predicament. Brian heard Gary scoot over beside him. He reached out a hand, touching to make sure Brian was there.

"It was Odie what done it," Gary said.

"Done what?"

"He killed Grampa. Told me he did."

Brian shook his head. "Why?"

"He found out about the gold," Gary answered. "He laughed—you know, that loud, ugly laugh of his. He told me how he done it. He hid at Grampa's fishing spot and waited for him. When Grampa got there, Odie hit him with a club, then pushed him into the lake. Then he put his fishing stuff out so it would look like he'd had a fishing accident. That's why stuff wasn't set out right, 'cause Odie done it. He didn't know how Grampa set his fishing stuff up." Gary made a gulping sound when he swallowed. "You know that tire track with the chunk cut out of it?"

"Yes."

111

"It was Odie's patrol car. He keeps it locked in the police barn. That's why we didn't find it them two days we spent looking at all the tires in Medicine Park."

Gary stopped talking.

"Why did he do that?" Brian wondered out loud. "Grampa never done nothin' to him. Why would he do somethin' like that?"

"Just pure old greed," Mrs. Becker answered with a sigh. "Lots of folks is like that. Greedy. Some worse than others. I figure Odie's bad as they come.

"He knew about that gold for a long time. That was the only failing my Chancy and Gary's grandpa had. They was a couple of talkie old cusses. I reckon half the folks in the county knew they was hunting for this gold. Most thought they was just a couple of crazy old men, and they figured there wasn't any gold to begin with. Others . . . well, they might have believed there was gold hidden in these mountains, but they never figured those two old men would ever find it.

"Odie . . . well, I reckon he was just so cussed greedy, he believed there *was* gold. And he had enough patience to wait around until Gary's grandpa found it. Then he killed him so he could get his maps."

Brian could hear Mrs. Becker crying. She sniffed back her tears and went on. "Wouldn't surprise me if Odie was the one who shot my Chancy in the back. Remember I told you somebody broke into my house right after Chancy died? I bet it was Odie trying to find his maps. That Odie's a mean, sneakin' devil if there ever was one."

Suddenly, light flooded the cave. There was a loud, ugly laugh. Brian looked up and saw Odie's sneering face glare down at them.

"You folks talking unkindly about me?" he taunted. "Ought to be ashamed of yourselves." He tossed the rope down. Then the nylon twine. "Get back to work," he roared. "It's raining outside like it ain't never gonna quit. I want to get this gold out of here 'fore the trails wash out between here and the road."

Mrs. Becker got to her feet. Angry, she put her hands on her hips and glared up at him. "What if we don't feel like workin' no more?" she snapped.

Odie only laughed. "Oh, you will," he answered.

"Just why will we?" Mrs. Becker snapped.

Odie set the lantern down on the edge of the pit. " 'Cause if you don't, I'm gonna shoot you."

Brian felt a tremble of fear shoot through his arms. He swallowed hard.

Mrs. Becker stood there glaring up at Odie. "The way I figure it, you're gonna kill us anyway. I don't see no sense helpin' you. Go ahead. Shoot us."

Odie didn't get mad over her dare. He only laughed. "I'd rather not. You see, if you load the gold for me, I won't have to shoot you. I'll just go off and leave you here. That's a promise."

A bitter sneer came over Mrs. Becker's wrinkled face.

"I'd just as soon be shot as left here to die of thirst and starvation."

Odie's voice was serious when he answered, "At least you'd have a chance. You might get lucky—might find a way out in a day or so—after I'm long gone. If you're alive, that is. If you got a bullet in you, there ain't no chance. No chance at all."

Mrs. Becker stood there thinking over what he'd said. Finally, she started toward the gold, motioning for Brian and Gary to come help.

Odie's long, ugly laugh roared from above. It echoed through the huge cave, making the rock shake and tremble with disgust. Brian cringed.

The twisted skeletons and the dead spirits of the Snake Dancers seemed kind and loving compared with Odie Ralston. Almost friendly, in fact.

Odie left again, to carry his gold outside the cave. When they were alone, Mrs. Becker got her flashlight out from under her skirt and shined it around the pit.

It looked hopeless. The walls that surrounded them were just too smooth for climbing. The edge of it was too far above for them to ever reach. They huddled together near the side of the pit. Quiet for a time. Thinking.

"Maybe we could get a rock and dig footholds in the side of the walls," Gary said.

Even in the dark, Brian could sense Mrs. Becker shaking her head. "We don't have any rocks," she said. "Only thing down here in this pit is us and those boxes."

"We could use the nails out of the boxes," Gary answered. "They'd be better for digging than a rock, anyhow."

"Ain't no nails," Mrs. Becker said. "Them boxes are so old, they're put together with wood pegs instead of nails. That pine in the boxes ain't near hard enough to even put a dent in this granite stone." She let out a long, thoughtful sigh. "Even if we did have a rock, or something to dig hand-holds with, it'd take us at least five days to reach the top of this thing. We couldn't go that long without water."

Brian felt his eyes pop open. A smile came. "I've got an idea," he said. "We could make us a ladder."

"A ladder?"

"Yeah. We could break one of those boxes apart and make us a ladder."

"We ain't got no nails," Gary argued.

"Don't need nails." Brian smiled. "We can tear strips of cloth off our shirts and tie the wood together with them. Use our belts, too."

"Might work," Mrs. Becker whispered. "Just might."

115

Brian was feeling real proud of himself for figuring a way out, when he heard Mrs. Becker let out a long, heavy sigh. "I'm afraid it'd still take too long," she said. "Three to four days. We could make it without food that long, but not without water. There's got to be another way."

There was a funny sound beside them.

"Hey!" Gary yelped. Then he almost laughed. "Don't worry about the water," he chuckled. "We got it."

"What?"

"Water," Gary repeated. "We got water. Feel over here. On the floor."

Brian reached out a hand. The floor of the pit felt cold. But the bare rock wasn't wet. It wasn't even damp.

"I don't feel nothin'," he answered.

"Over here by me," Gary said.

Brian crawled toward Gary's voice. Mrs. Becker clicked her flashlight on about the time Brian got to where Gary was.

Gary was near the middle of the pit. And sure enough, there beside him was a tiny pool of water. He smiled up at Brian and Mrs. Becker, flicking the water with his fingers.

"See? It ain't much, but maybe it'd be enough to last for a little bit."

Brian smiled. Inside, he'd been praying for water. Now it was like his prayers had been answered. He turned quickly to Mrs. Becker. He expected her to be smiling. She wasn't!

Before he knew it, Mrs. Becker was on her feet. She rushed over beside them. When she shined the light on the little pool of water, the reflections from the water danced around the walls of the pit, making funny patterns on the walls. They were like whining, shimmering white ghosts dancing about the rock. Mrs. Becker looked at the pool for a long time. She moved the light around, trying to find where the water was coming from.

Brian couldn't understand the worry on her face. He figured she would be happy about the water. After all, wasn't that what she had been wanting? Now that they had water, she wouldn't have to worry about them dying of thirst. They'd have time to make their wood ladder. They'd have time to get out of the pit.

Mrs. Becker kept moving the light about the walls and sides of the pit. Brian scratched at his head. "What is it, Mrs. Becker? How come you look so—"

"Hush," she cut him off sharply.

"Why, what is it?"

"Hush," she snapped again. "Listen!"

They were quiet at once. Listening. Holding their breath. The dead silence of the dark cave swept in on them.

Then, suddenly, the silence was broken.

There was a faint plopping sound. The plop-plunk of water, like the large drops that fall from a leaky faucet in a bathtub.

Brian waited. Listened. The sound came again. Then again. Mrs. Becker turned her light on the pool of water beside them. Ripples raced out from the center in tiny circles that raced away from where the drop had fallen.

The next drop of water came sooner than the other. It made the little pool ripple again before it got still. Then another drop came.

Mrs. Becker turned her light toward the top of the pit. The edge of the pit was at least fifteen feet above them. The top of the cave was another ten feet beyond that. Like the rest of the cave, the roof here was honeycombed with the small, round holes. Mrs. Becker kept moving her light around. She looked at one hole, then another.

Finally, a drop of water caught Brian's eye. Mrs. Becker's light made it sparkle. It fell from the lip of a large hole in the roof of the cave. Came straight down and landed with a plip-plop in their pool.

The drops that fell were coming faster. Mrs. Becker moaned. "I should have known," she said. "It's a sinkhole!"

"A what?" Brian asked.

Mrs. Becker turned the light on him. It made him blink. "This is a sinkhole," she repeated. "A pit carved out of solid rock by falling water. The rain outside seeps into the rocks and finally works its way down to those holes. After thousands of years it's hollowed out this pit we're trapped in."

Brian smiled. "Good. With that water coming

in, we'll have enough to drink. We won't die of thirst. We can make a ladder and get out of here."

The glare from Mrs. Becker's flashlight hit his eyes again. "You don't understand," she snapped. "We're trapped. If it keeps raining, this thing will fill up. It'll fill up just like a well. We'll drown! Like a bunch of rats trapped in a well—we'll drown!"

Brian felt a sick, sinking feeling inside. He'd never felt so hopeless. So lost.

The drops fell faster and faster, one after another, until it sounded more like a stream of water than falling drops. Their little pool of water began to grow—larger and deeper, until it all but covered the floor of the pit.

They scooted back, pressing against the smooth walls at the edge. Brian knew now that this pit was a death trap. There was no way out.

CHAPTER 13

Light came from above. It was faint at first, but grew brighter. The last ray of hope in a dark, cold, wet world.

Gary started yelling. "Help us!" he screamed. "Down here. Help us. Please!"

Brian found himself on his feet. He was yelling, too. Begging. Pleading for help. "Get us out of here. Hurry! Don't let us drown. Help!"

The water was just below his knees. It tugged at his feet and legs. Made it hard to move. The light came closer. At last a lantern shone down from the edge of the pit. Then Odie Ralston leaned out over the edge. He glared down at them.

"Help us," Brian begged. "Please let us out!"

Odie studied the situation for a moment. Then

he rocked back on his heels and stuck out his fat stomach. His loud, evil laugh drowned out the sound of the falling water.

The hole in the roof of the cave seemed to grow wider by the second. Water first fell in drops—faster and faster, until the drops became a trickle. Then a stream. Now it was pouring through the hole. Bubbling and churning the water already in the middle of the pit. Growing deeper by the second.

Mrs. Becker had been quiet. She looked up at Odie Ralston and clasped her hands together. "Help the boys," she pleaded. "They never done anything to hurt you. My life don't matter. But don't let them die down here in this pit. Help them! Please!"

Odie only chuckled.

Mrs. Becker's eyes scrunched up angrily. "Doesn't life mean anything to you, Odie Ralston? They're just children. They can't harm you. Get them out of here."

Odie's laugh rocked the cave. "Those boys don't mean nothin'," he sneered. "I was worrying how I was gonna get rid of all three of you anyway. Now I ain't got to worry no more." He knelt down and looked over the edge of the pit at them.

"You see," he explained, "I was in such a hurry I left most of those maps back at your house, Gary. The way I see it, sooner or later, your folks are gonna figure you found your grandpa's maps and went looking for the gold. The chances are pretty slim, but they might find you before you starve to death. Then you'll tell 'em I was the one that killed the old man.''

"We won't tell, Odie," Brian promised. "I swear, we won't tell. Just get us out of here."

Odie ignored him. "I didn't want to shoot you, neither," he went on. "People find you shot full of holes, they never would stop looking for your murderer. But this way, folks won't never know there was anyone else around. They'll think you come in here looking for that gold. Got yourselves trapped and died sort of natural-like. I couldn't have planned it better if I'd tried."

He laughed and raised his lantern so he could see the water pouring in through the roof of the cave. He laughed again.

"What about the gold?" Mrs. Becker screamed up at him. "If you let the boys out, I'll send up the rest of the gold for you. Otherwise, it'll stay down here with us. You'll never get it."

That brought a frown to Odie's face. He thought on it a minute, then shrugged. "There's only about a couple of thousand dollars' worth left in that big box. Besides, those two pack-horses I got tied up at the foot of the hill are so loaded down now they can barely stand. I don't need the rest of the gold."

The water was halfway to Brian's waist now. It was hard to stand, hard to keep his footing.

Odie shined his lantern on them. "I'd like to

stick around and watch." He chuckled. "But I'd best be going." He smiled, real proud of himself. "You two boys see how long you can hold your breath when you finally go under," he roared out. "I can almost see it. You'll suck in a good deep breath. Hold it till your lungs are about to burst— then it'll be all over."

The light from his lantern turned away. Brian could hear him chuckling as he walked away, leaving them there to drown.

"I hope the Lord gives you exactly what you deserve, Odie Ralston," Mrs. Becker raged at him. "I hope you spend the rest of eternity burning in the fires of—"

She broke off then, trembling. Brian watched as she bowed her head and cried.

"Forgive me, dear Lord," she whispered. "I spoke in anger. I didn't mean what I said. Please forgive me."

Brian went to her. He put his arms around her and tried to comfort her.

"It's all right, Mrs. Becker. Don't cry. Please."

She seemed to calm down some then. She got the flashlight out and looked around. The hole in the roof had grown wider and wider, letting in more water every second. It thundered and roared like a waterfall as it plunged into the pit.

Brian could feel it swirling around his waist. He and Gary clung to each other. Mrs. Becker held them both wrapped in her arms.

It wasn't long before Brian felt the water up

around his chest. They didn't have much time left. Soon it would all be over.

There was a sound then. A sound that came above the loud roar of the falling water. A strange, eerie sound that set the hair tingling on the back of Brian's neck.

It was a scream. A shrill, painful, terrified scream. A scream of agony and fear. It came from far off in the cave. Brian listened. Wondered.

The sound of screaming came again. This time, it was followed by the loud crack of gunfire. The crack of the shots came again and again.

"What on earth . . . " Mrs. Becker whispered.

There was a moment of silence. Then another scream. It was Odie's scream. A scream filled with terror. A scream so cold and frightening, Brian knew he would remember the sound of it forever.

Suddenly, Brian felt something at his side. It was cold and hard, like a hand tugging at his arm. It startled him. He jumped, falling in the deep water.

The water swirled over him. He struggled. Fought his way back to the surface. Mrs. Becker reached out. Caught him by an arm. Pulled him back to her.

The water was up to his neck now. Mrs. Becker pulled him close. She held him up from the water until he stopped coughing and sputtering.

"What is it?" she asked. "Why did you jump?"

Brian swallowed the last bit of water in his throat and coughed again. "Something grabbed me. It felt like a hand, only it was real cold."

Mrs. Becker had turned her light off. None of them wanted to watch the water rising to swallow them. So they had stood in the dark, just waiting. She turned the light on, holding it above her head to keep it out of the water.

They looked around for a long time, searching the swirling water to find what had hit Brian's arm. Finally, they found it.

"Look! There!" Mrs. Becker gasped. "That's what grabbed you!"

Brian saw what she was pointing at. It was the box that the gold was in. Only Brian knew that wasn't what had grabbed his arm. Right before it grabbed him, he had felt a cold breath on the back of his neck—felt eyes watching him. But whatever it had been was gone now.

CHAPTER 14

The huge wooden box floated beside them. The top, just barely above the water, was held low in the pool by the sacks of gold that remained in the bottom. It moved back and forth, pushed around by the splashing roar of the falling water.

"The box," Mrs. Becker yelped. "It's floating. It's our last chance."

The box was so low in the water, and it moved so silently around the pit, that they might never have seen it. Only Brian knew they were meant to find it. That was what the hand on his arm was doing. It was trying to lead him to the box.

Mrs. Becker moved toward it quickly. She held Brian by the waist and lifted him near it. "See if you can reach down and get those gold sacks out," she said. "But be careful. If it tips over it'll fill with water and sink."

Brian was careful not to lean on the edge of the box when Mrs. Becker lifted him beside it. He could tell that the old woman was having no trouble lifting him. Even though he was pretty heavy, most of his weight was supported by the water.

Odie Ralston could only carry eight sacks at a time, but Brian had lost count of the trips he had made. Now there were only a few sacks left in the bottom of the wooden crate. With each one Brian lifted out, the box rose higher in the water.

Behind him, he heard Mrs. Becker cough. He glanced over his shoulder. The water in the pit had risen to her neck, then her chin. They didn't have much time.

It was tricky work. Brian had to hurry. He knew if he hurried too much, he might get careless. If he got careless, he might let the box tip and the water would rush in. Without the old wooden box, they didn't stand a chance.

He forced himself to move slowly, to make sure he had a good hold on each of the heavy sacks before he lifted them over the side and dropped them into the bubbling, swirling water.

Mrs. Becker coughed again. "Gary! Hang on," she sputtered. "Brian?"

"Yes, ma'am," he answered.

"Take the light. I don't want it to get wet. I gotta use my other hand to get Gary."

The bottom of the box was dry. Brian dropped

the light. He reached for another sack of gold and dropped it into the water.

"Gary!" Mrs. Becker screamed. "Gary!"

Her shout startled Brian. He almost lost his balance. When he looked back, Gary was gone. He had been holding on to Mrs. Becker's shoulder, but he wasn't there now.

Mrs. Becker was looking around, frantic and scared. "Brian!" she shouted above the roar of the water. "Can you hold to the box without tipping it? Gary lost his grip on me. He went under!"

Without answering, Brian grabbed the edge of the box and took his weight from Mrs. Becker's arms. She moved away. Her mouth barely above the water, she reached out, searching with her hands.

Brian heard a choking cough from the far side of the pit. Then Gary's voice came. He tried to yell "Help," but only managed to get half the word out before he was choked off by the water.

The small hole in the roof of the cave had grown to a large, yawning mouth. Water poured down from it—enough so that the whole pool churned and bubbled. The currents were like lead weights on Brian's feet. They pulled and tugged, trying to yank him loose from the box, trying to drag him under. He could imagine what it was like for Gary without anything to hold to.

"Gary!" Mrs. Becker screamed. "Brian! Shine the light over here. I can't see."

Brian had wanted both hands free so he could get the gold out of the box faster. He pulled his chin up to the edge of the crate. The light was still on. But down in the bottom of the box like it was, he knew he could never reach it.

"Brian," Mrs. Becker screamed again. "The light. Quick. He's gone under."

Brian closed his eyes. But there wasn't time for a prayer. He gave a hard kick with both feet. Pulled himself up.

It was a risky move. Powerful risky. If he tipped the box, he and Mrs. Becker would have no chance against the whirling water. Without the light, Mrs. Becker might not find Gary in time. He had to risk it. No matter what might happen to him, he couldn't let his friend drown.

It worked. He pulled up to the edge of the box and flipped himself over. Water spilled in behind him. The box rocked violently from side to side. Then it settled.

Once inside the box, Brian was careful when he got the light and crawled to his knees. He was lucky the box hadn't turned. Lucky more water hadn't come—enough to sink their last chance of survival.

He shined the light all around the cave. Mrs. Becker was having trouble moving through the water. It was above her chin now. She had to bounce to keep her head above the raging torrent.

Then he saw Gary. Not really Gary, but his

flailing, struggling arms where the water had pulled him under.

"Over there," he shouted, holding the light where Gary had gone.

Mrs. Becker moved to the spot. She reached out, grabbing a handful of Gary's hair. He came up, coughing and sputtering. Water streamed from his mouth.

Mrs. Becker had to struggle just to hold him up. The flood of water pouring into the pit grew deeper by the second. When Mrs. Becker held Gary up, she went down. She would hold him up for a long time, then bob back to the surface for a quick breath of air. But when she lifted Gary, water came just above her eyes.

Brian knew she could never make it back. Quickly, he put the light down. Fast as he could, he heaved sack after heavy sack of gold over the edge of the box.

Finally, when it was all gone, the box floated high in the water. He had to strain to reach the pool with his hands. Careful not to bring the box under the pouring water from the top of the cave, he paddled with his hands. He moved the box around to where Mrs. Becker was struggling with Gary.

Gary was groggy from all the water he'd sucked in. When he saw the box, he lunged for it. Brian leaned quickly to the other side. The box tipped toward Gary, but Brian had moved fast enough to balance the weight.

"Careful," he screamed. "Don't tip us. Can you get in?"

Gary coughed. "I think. You ready?"

Brian got a good hold on the edge of the box. It leaned and bobbed in the water. Brian had to hang far out over the edge to keep it flat. When Gary flung his leg over the edge and rolled into the bottom, Brian had to jump back quickly into the center.

Gary gasped for air. He belched out big mouthfuls of the water he'd swallowed. The box tipped a little when Mrs. Becker caught the edge.

"He all right?"

"I think," Brian nodded. "Can you get in?"

"Don't know," she coughed. "Can't touch the bottom. Nothin' to push off of."

The box was sitting a little deeper in the water with Gary's added weight. When Mrs. Becker tried to pull herself in from the side, it tipped way over. Water came less than an inch from the edge. She let down quick. The box rocked, but no more water got in.

Brian moved to the other side. "Try it now," he called.

Brian leaned far out over the edge, hoping he could help balance her weight. But again the box leaned far to the side. Mrs. Becker had to let go before the water rushed in to fill their crude life raft.

"It's no use," she gasped. "I'm too heavy. I'll

tip it over. You and Gary stay in the middle. I'll hang on to the side here."

Brian could hear the weakness in her voice. She had struggled hard to rescue Gary. Now she was tired—almost exhausted. He realized she wouldn't be able to hang on long. The cold water was churning and pulling her down. Tired as she was, if she didn't make it into the box soon, she'd slip and be swept under by the whirlpool.

There had to be a way. There just had to.

Suddenly, there was a jarring bump. Brian lost his balance on the slick wood floor. He tumbled over Gary and struggled to his knees. He shined the light around, trying to see what had happened.

The box had floated over to the side of the pit. When it bumped into the rock wall, it had sent him tumbling clear to the far end. Again, Brian knew someone was helping. Someone—or something—had given him the answer.

He reached out and got Gary's arm, helping him to the end of the box where he had landed.

"Mrs. Becker?"

"Yes, Brian." Her voice came even weaker than before.

Brian pressed himself against the far end of the box. He pulled Gary tight against it with him.

"We're down at the end of the box, Mrs. Becker. Try coming over the far end. It's less likely to tip that way."

"I don't know if I can, Brian."

"You've got to! Now, hurry!"

"What if I turn you over?" she argued weakly.

"You won't. I'm sure. Now, hurry!"

He could feel the box jiggling as she moved around to the far end. When he could tell she was there, he leaned back as far as he could.

"Push up hard, Mrs. Becker," he urged. "Come up on your arms, and then just tumble into the bottom."

It worked! The old wooden box bounced and tipped in the water. It rocked from side to side—bobbed up and down like a wild teeter-totter. But it didn't turn over. Some water came in, but not much. In a minute or so, it settled and floated smoothly like a lily pad on the surface of a pond.

Mrs. Becker lay gasping for air in the bottom. Gary coughed and belched water a few more times. But after a while, he was able to sit up. Brian sat in the center. He put his hands over the edge and paddled with them. That way he could keep the box near the edge of the pit. If they floated out into the center, where the funnel of water poured down from the roof of the cave, it'd sink them for sure.

Brian was scared for Mrs. Becker. She was tired and had been through a terrible strain. Finally, she was able to get up on her good knee and help him and Gary keep the box near the edge of the pit.

"We're gonna be all right, now." Brian smiled. "We made it. We're safe now."

Mrs. Becker glanced over her shoulder at him. "Maybe."

He felt himself frown, not understanding. "What do you mean, maybe? We got in the box without tipping it. We're safe now."

"For how long?" she snapped at him. Then she paused for a moment. "I'm sorry I yelled at you," she said in a soft voice. "I don't want to cause you to worry—but I figure you're old enough to know the truth."

Brian leaned toward her. He tilted his head to the side, wondering.

"What truth?"

Mrs. Becker's rounded shoulders slumped. "We're still in this cursed pit. Only instead of being on dry, solid ground, we're in this box. An old, old box. The wood's half rotted and loose. It's gonna soak up water like a sponge. Those other boxes didn't even float."

She turned to look at him. The worry and sorrow burned deep into her tired, old eyes. "This old crate won't float for long. In this cave—without the sun to help evaporate it—the water in this pit could stand for months. Years. Only now we can't use this box for a ladder." She sighed. A tear rolled down her wrinkled cheek. Brian could tell the tear was for him and Gary—not herself. "We're still trapped, boys. Trapped even worse than before."

CHAPTER 15

The seconds rolled by, turning to minutes and then to hours. Brian couldn't get over it. He'd been so sure they were safe, so sure that once they made it into the big wooden box they would be all right.

But when he realized what Mrs. Becker said was true, he felt cold inside. Cold and empty, like all the hope and courage that he felt before had been swept away and there was nothing left.

Mrs. Becker slumped against one end of the box. She was tired—plumb tuckered out. Now she lay restless, just on the edge of uneasy sleep. Behind him, Gary lay at the other end. He'd come as close to drowning as Brian had seen anyone come. It had taken a lot out of him. And although he didn't sleep, his eyes were closed and his breathing was light.

After Brian was sure they were all right, he clicked the flashlight off. He slumped against the side of the box. Waited.

The water kept pouring in from the roof of the cave. The box set lower and lower with the passing of time. Already he could feel that the boards near the bottom were wet. Just like Mrs. Becker had said, the crate was soaking up water like a sponge.

Brian closed his eyes. Only he couldn't sleep. Someone had to make sure the box didn't float under the pouring water. Besides, too many things kept rolling across his mind. There were too many unanswered questions to think about.

Why did Odie scream? What had happened to him to make him yell out with that terrified, frightening scream? Why was I so sure a hand touched me, in the water? It might have been the box bouncing against me. So why was I sure it was a hand? What did the old Indian legend mean about "the evil that lives inside the mountain"? Was it this pit? Or was it something else? Why did . . .

His thinking suddenly ended. There was a loud roar. The box rocked from side to side, almost spilling them out. Water splashed. Brian could feel the cold, wet spray against his face.

"Brian? Gary?" Mrs. Becker yelled out.

"What . . . ?" Gary shrieked.

Brian grabbed up the light. He clicked it on. Made sure Gary and Mrs. Becker were still with him. Then he looked around to see what had happened. Finally, he found it. Another hole had opened in the roof of the cave. It was even bigger than the first hole. The water poured down from it with a deafening roar. It made the pool slosh and churn.

All three had to paddle hard to keep from being swept under it. Brian stopped for a second to look at it again with his light. This time, there was a third hole. It was at the far side of the pit. More water was pouring in.

Suddenly, something caught his eye. He turned the light and looked to the side. It was the edge of the pit. It was right there, only a foot or two above them.

After all the time they'd spent down there—after all the water that had poured in—the wooden box had gone up with it. Right to the edge of the pit. Brian started to call out to Gary and Mrs. Becker. He wanted to tell them that they could get out, now, that they were safe.

The words never got out of his throat.

There was a rumbling sound. Far off at first, but growing louder by the second. Even the water where they floated seemed to tremble and shake. Then, all at once, the whole back of the cave seemed to crumble.

The three holes in the roof above them seemed to flow together. The water merged into a solid wall of white, foaming spray. Rocks fell away behind them. The wall opened up, pushed aside by a wall of water that came growling and tumbling toward their little raft.

There wasn't time for anything. The water hit them, rocking the box from side to side, tipping it back and forth. All Brian could do was grab hold of the sides. He hung on for his life.

Mrs. Becker screamed. Gary yelled something, but Brian couldn't hear him. Then they were moving. Brian could feel it. It was as if they were being pushed along with the water, instead of being swept under by it, like he figured they would be.

They were moving fast. A falling, rocking sensation—like riding in a boat down the rapids.

Brian reached to his lap where he had dropped the flashlight. The movement of the boat slowed, and he was able to look around with the light.

They were no longer in the pit. In fact, Brian realized they weren't even in the same cavern where the pit had been. They were in the room where he had seen the pictures painted on the wall.

The room was wide and flat, allowing the wall of water that had pushed them from the pit to slow some.

Brian moved the light around. The dry bones of the skeletons floated everywhere. The skull of one made a clicking sound as it bounced against the box that carried them. Brian shined the light back where he'd seen the huge Indian. Water poured from the tunnel between his feet.

He moved the light to look in front of them. The water was carrying them toward another tunnel. He remembered it was the steep, narrow one that led to the big cavern just before the entrance.

He started to yell for Mrs. Becker and Gary to hang on. There wasn't time. The water narrowed its channel as it flowed into the tunnel. They were flying down through the dark, narrow passage with the speed of the wind itself.

Brian dropped the light again when he reached to hold on to the edges. In the dark, it was like falling. Like falling into a black, bottomless pit. Falling faster and faster. He braced himself, expecting them to crash into the wall at any second.

Instead of slamming and splintering against the walls of the cave, the box slowed gradually. There was a strange buzzing sound. Almost a rattling hum.

Brian grabbed for the light again as they slowed. The sound grew louder.

They were in the big cavern. The trough that Brian had followed into the cave was filled with water. Like a river, it wound and twisted its way through the big room.

Brian let go of the box with his other hand. He stuck his finger in his ear and shook it around. The buzzing sound kept growing louder and louder. It was almost deafening. The musky smell he had first noticed when he came into the cave was there, too. Thick and heavy, it seemed to fill the air. The sound was worse. Louder every second.

Brian gritted his teeth. He wished the sound would stop before his ears busted. The buzzing grew louder. Then . . . Brian saw what was making the sound.

His insides seemed to freeze. He couldn't breathe. The goose bumps popped up all over him. His eyes acted like they were stuck—wide open and unable to even blink.

This was the part of the cave that was honeycombed with all the small, round holes. And here, the cave suddenly came alive. Breathing, rattling, hissing sounds came from everywhere. Movement all about them. Crawling, twining, striking movement that made the whole cave seem alive—like some giant, sprawling monster.

"Rattlesnakes!" Mrs. Becker breathed. "Keep your arms in the box. Don't move. Don't even breathe."

Brian knew this was the evil of the Snake Dancer's Cave. Rattlesnakes. Thousands of the slithering, red-eyed monsters. This was the evil that lived inside the mountain. The whole cave was one gigantic rattlesnake den. The snakes had probably spent the winter in the thousands of tiny, round holes that honeycombed the walls. When the warm spring rain had come, they'd had to crawl out into the big cave to escape the wet.

They were everywhere now. Slithering, wiggling bodies that tangled and wrapped about each other. The buzzing sound became a distinct rattling. Their tails were whipping back and forth from side to side.

Some crawled from the holes in the walls. But most were already out in the cave. They lined the banks of the little channel where the box floated—only a few feet away as Brian and the others passed.

Brian wanted to yank the light back. Duck down inside the bottom of the box. Only he remembered what Mrs. Becker had said: *Don't move. Don't even breathe.*

So he sat like a statue as they floated past hundreds of snakes—thousands. The sight was enough to turn his stomach. His head seemed to spin.

The snakes hissed and rattled and struck at one another. They crawled about, as thick as the prairie grass. Slithering, twining, twisting. The spiny scales over their eyes were almost like horns—like the horns of the devil himself.

The shivers caught Brian. He tried to keep from shaking and trembling all over. He couldn't. The cold, icy feeling started low in his stomach. It spread all over him, until he was trembling from head to toe. He couldn't stand it much longer, couldn't stand being in the cave with the ugly, slimy, crawly rattlesnakes all around. If Brian didn't get away from them soon, he knew his insides were going to bust wide open.

All at once, they were flying again. The water

had flowed into the narrow opening of the entrance tunnel. They were rushed along with the white water. Down! Down! Then, suddenly, up and out. Out into the black night.

Brian didn't know where he was. He didn't know what had happened. He felt the water fall away from the bottom of their box. For a split second, they seemed to hang motionless in the air.

Then they fell. Straight down. Straight down into the nothingness of empty space. Suddenly, they slammed down into something. They hit with a bone-jarring crunch that shattered the wooden box.

The jarring slammed up Brian's back. Into his head. He blinked. Fought to keep his eyes open. His head spun. And when the force of his landing knocked him out—right before he slumped unconscious to the ground—he was sure that he was dead.

CHAPTER 16

Brian was afraid to open his eyes. He was scared he might still be in the cave, surrounded by the slimy, crawling rattlesnakes. He lay there for a long time, awake, but with his eyes closed tight. There were voices. Far-off voices, like those heard in a dream.

He felt warm. Then there was a soft, gentle hand on his forehead. He blinked. It was light all around. He blinked again, then forced his eyes to stay open.

Mama was there. She knelt over him and smiled when he opened his eyes to look up at her.

"Are you all right?"

Brian smiled back. "I don't know. Where am I? What . . ."

Mama helped him sit up. They were beside the

pool of water in the Valley of the Snake Dancer.

For a minute, Brian thought it had all been an ugly nightmare. The strange, horrible things that had happened didn't really happen at all. But when he looked around and saw where they were, he knew it hadn't been a dream.

He jerked, twisting around to look at the mouth of the cave. What if the snakes had come out during the night? What if they had followed them?

Then, suddenly, he realized that the cave wasn't there. His mouth dropped open. He pointed.

"What . . . where's the cave?"

Dad was beside him now, too. He looked at where Brian was pointing and put a firm hand on his shoulder. "It's gone, son. Gone forever."

"But . . . how . . . what happend? It was there . . ." Brian couldn't make himself stop stuttering.

Dad patted his shoulder again, trying to calm him. "After we were sure you were all right, some of us men went up there—where Mrs. Becker told us the cave was. There was a fresh cut in the rock, like lightning had struck just above the cave. A few of the men claim they saw the flash, right before daybreak, while they were working their way up the cliff. I bet there's five ton of rocks blocking the entrance to that place."

Brian looked at the slabs of rock where the mouth of the cave had once been. It was a pretty sight. It was a good feeling to know the cave was closed up—the evil locked away forever inside the mountain.

Mama hugged him up close. "Mrs. Becker told us everything," she said. "What a horrible experience you've been through. I can't imagine anything so terrible happening to my little boy. I should never have left you alone last night. My poor honey."

Brian felt his nose crinkle up. This was just too much mush for any eleven-year-old boy to stand. He pushed away from her and looked around.

"Gary? Mrs. Becker? Are they all right?"

Dad got his arm and helped him to his feet. "Gary's got a broken arm. His dad and some of the others carried him down the mountain and took him to the doctor in Lawton."

Brian sighed, knowing that Gary was all right. "What about Mrs. Becker?"

Dad shook his head. "I'll tell you," he smirked. "That old lady must be as tough as a boot. She don't even have a scratch on her."

"Are you sure she's all right?" Brian urged.

Dad smiled. "Look for yourself."

He pointed to a large group of people. They were all clumped around Mrs. Becker. She was sitting on a rock and chatting away with them like she'd known them all her life.

Some of the people at the edge of the group noticed Brian was awake and on his feet. They came rushing over and crowded around him to see if he could add anything to the fabulous tale Mrs. Becker had told them.

But Dad wouldn't have any part of their questions. "I'm sorry, folks," he said firmly. "This boy's been through too much. He needs to rest." He patted Brian on the shoulder. "Come on. Let's go home."

The walk back down the mountain didn't seem hard at all. Every time Brian got to a steep part, there was always somebody there, anxious to help him.

The crowd, near the barbed-wire fence where Mrs. Becker had wrecked the motorcycle, had seen two horses come wandering out of the woods. The horses were all lathered up in a sweat, like they'd been running. They had big canvas saddlepacks on their backs, but the packs were ripped open and empty.

"Looks like they been running all over these mountains," one man said.

"Must have run up against dead trees and rocks," another called. "These packs are ripped all over. Ain't nothin' inside."

"Wonder what was in them," a woman asked.

Brian felt his eyes flash. He looked toward Mrs. Becker. She held her fingers to her lips. Brian nodded, agreeing with her. The curse of the Snake Dancer's Gold *was* true. If they told about the gold, there would be more people looking for it. More trouble. It was a secret Brian knew that the three of them would keep until their dying day.

When they reached the road, it looked like there were fifty cars or more parked along the roadway. Like everybody in Medicine Park had turned out to help search for them.

Right before Brian got in the car to go home, he turned to look at the mountain. Even with all these people, it was hard to believe they'd been found. The Valley of the Snake Dancer was hidden far back in the hills—a place where nobody ever went.

With a puzzled frown, Brian turned to Dad. "How did you find us?"

Dad looked real serious. He gave his head a little jerk to the side. "It was Odie Ralston," he answered.

Mama rushed up beside him. "Oh, Charles. Don't talk about that. It's too horrible. Don't tell him."

Brian tugged at his arm. "Please, Dad. I've got to know."

Dad swallowed hard and closed his eyes. "We got home about midnight last night. When we went into Gary's house we could tell something had happened. We saw where there had been a struggle. Gary's mother got on the telephone, and within an hour folks came from all over, to help us look for you."

Brian waved a hand, cutting him off. "But what

about Odie? Did you catch him? Did he tell you what happened?"

Dad looked down at the ground and shook his head. "No. We found him lying dead, here in the road. He'd been snake-bit. There must have been fifty fang marks all over him. We also found the maps, the rice paper, and Grampa's letter in his pocket. The water must have washed his body down from the cave. After we found him, we followed the stream bed until we found you. I just thank God you weren't hurt, that you're alive and well. Now, come on. Let's go home."

There were still a lot of questions left in Brian's head, questions like: What made him so sure a hand had touched him, back in the cave? Why had the box jammed against the wall just at the right time to help him figure out a way to get Mrs. Becker into it? Why, of all the places it could have hit, did a bolt of lightning strike just above the mouth of Death Cave?

Brian frowned, puzzling over all the questions for a minute. And as he did, it came to him that they were questions which might never be answered, no matter how much he thought about them.

For now, it was enough to know that Gary and Mrs. Becker and he were safe and happy. It was good to know the cave was closed off by tons of rock and the slimy, ugly rattlesnakes were locked away for good.

The hum of the motor and the movement of the

car felt good as they drove back home. The seat was soft against his back, and Mama's shoulder was smooth and comfortable against his cheek. It didn't take long before he was asleep.

On Sunday afternoon, after church and before Brian and his folks had to pack the car for the drive back to their home in Chickasha, there was a big party for Mrs. Becker.

Gary's mom was the one who got it started, but it seemed like almost everybody in Medicine Park showed up. When people found out what she did to rescue Gary from Odie Ralston, they all wanted to come and thank her.

The women brought sandwiches and pies and cakes. While they were setting stuff up on tables on Mrs. Becker's front lawn, the men brought paint and brushes and started giving her crusty-looking old house a new coat of paint.

Folks weren't afraid of her, now that they understood why she'd spent so many years being a hermit. They could almost understand how frightened she was, not knowing who had killed her husband and knowing someone was trying to steal the maps from his house.

It was a busy place. People were all over, everybody wanting to shake Mrs. Becker's hand and tell her how much they respected her, and invite her to their house for a visit or promise to come see her again real soon.

It was almost dark when Gary and Brian and

Mrs. Becker finally found a little time together away from the crowd of people. There was a dry spot around the corner of the porch where the men hadn't painted. When Brian and Gary saw Mrs. Becker sitting there alone, they went to join her.

"Not used to all these people," she admitted. "I'm plum tuckered out."

Gary nodded. "They been here almost all afternoon and don't act like they're ever gonna be ready to go home."

Mrs. Becker kind of chuckled. "Reckon if I got my ax out of the barn and started walking around carrying that, they'd go home?"

Brian laughed, knowing she really didn't mean it. "It sure got rid of me and Gary the first time we came up here."

They all laughed, remembering. They sat quietly for a time, watching all the people. Finally, Gary leaned forward. He motioned Mrs. Becker and Brian to come close. Talking in a real soft voice, he said, "I've heard a story about Jesse and Frank James. Them and their gang robbed a train and buried the loot up somewhere on Mount Scott. I reckon if the three of us was to get some maps and start looking . . ."

Brian and Mrs. Becker were sitting on either side of him. They looked at each other. They smiled and nodded their heads.

Then—they commenced beating up on Gary. It was a playful beating, not a real one. Mrs. Becker would clunk Gary on the head. Brian would punch him on the shoulder or act like he was going to bust him in the stomach.

They all laughed.

"I was just funning." Gary squalled like he was being killed. "I didn't really mean it."

"I've had enough treasure hunting to last me a lifetime," Mrs. Becker said as she thumped Gary on the head again.

"Me too," Brian agreed.

But something told him that, come summer vacation, when his folks brought him down to spend some time with Gary, the three of them would end up spending a lot of time up on Mount Scott.

About the Author

BILL WALLACE is an elementary school principal and physical education teacher who wrote *A Dog Called Kitty* and *Trapped in Death Cave* to entertain his fourth graders. He also keeps a pet boa constrictor at school as an assistant science teacher.

A Dog Called Kitty won the Texas Bluebonnet Award and the Oklahoma Sequoia Award after being chosen by children in those states as one of their favorite books.

Wallace, his wife Carol, and their three children live on a farm west of Chickasha, Oklahoma, with three dogs, two cats and two horses.